Witch Is Why Two Became One

Published by Implode Publishing Ltd
© Implode Publishing Ltd 2016

The right of Adele Abbott to be identified as the Author of the Work has been asserted by her in accordance with the Copyright, Designs and Patents Act 1988.

All rights reserved, worldwide.
No part of this publication may be reproduced, stored in a retrieval system, or transmitted, in any form or by any means without the prior written permission of the copyright owner.

The characters and events in this book are fictitious. Any similarity to real persons, dead or alive, is purely coincidental and not intended by the author.

Chapter 1

It was a beautiful morning, and all was well with the world.

What do you mean it makes a change for me to be happy and positive? Anyone would think I was a grouch.

Last Friday, Jack had come up with the idea of going away for a long weekend. I'd taken a bit of persuading because normally I liked to plan things well in advance. I don't do 'spontaneous'. We went to Filey where we stayed in a beautiful little B&B. The weather was great, and we had a fantastic time. I'd assumed we'd come back on the Monday, but Jack had booked a couple of days off work, so we stayed until Tuesday evening. The break had done me a power of good; I felt refreshed and ready for whatever the world could throw at me.

By the time I'd had my shower and dressed, Jack had already left for work. I was eating breakfast when my phone rang.

"Hi, Kathy!"

"Jill? You're out of the shower, then?"

"What do you mean?"

"I called earlier. Jack said he thought you'd taken up residence in there."

"Cheek! I wasn't in there that long."

"He tells me you had a great weekend?"

"We did. It was fantastic. I feel so much better for it."

"Good. Look, I just called back to check what time Jack planned to call around tomorrow night."

"Tomorrow night?"

"Didn't he tell you?"

"He'd left when I came downstairs." Then I spotted the

note on the breakfast bar. "Hold on a minute, he's left me a note." I quickly skimmed it. "We're babysitting?"

"Yeah. Jack sounded really enthusiastic."

"Did he? And the kids are coming over *here*?"

"Yeah. I assumed you'd want to come to our house, but Jack insisted that the kids should come to you. He said it would be an adventure for them."

I was going to kill Jack.

"So, what time will he be coming to collect them?" she asked.

"I don't know. I'll have to check with him tonight. Where are you and Peter going?"

"We've got tickets for the UK's number one pop sensation!"

"Pop sensation? You sound like a cheesy seventies DJ. Who is it, anyway?"

"Only Murray Murray!"

"Murray who?"

"Murray."

"Yeah I got that. What's his last name?"

"Murray."

"Now you've lost me. What's his first name?"

"Murray."

"So let me get this straight. His name is Murray Murray?"

"Yes. Don't tell me you haven't heard of him?"

"No. I think I'd remember if I had. What kind of name is that anyway?"

"Don't you ever listen to the radio, Jill?"

"Only the talk programs. I can't be doing with most of the music these days. It gives me a headache."

"You really are old before your time, aren't you?"

"If by that you mean that I have good taste in music, then I suppose you're right."

**

Megan was cleaning her van.

"Hi, Jill!" She called to me as soon as I stepped out of the door.

"Morning, Megan."

"Did you have a good weekend?"

"Great. What about you?"

"I've been working. And guess what? I've landed another four new clients. If it carries on at this rate, I'll soon be able to give up the modelling."

I considered mentioning Kathy's concerns that Megan was poaching Peter's clients, but then thought better of it. Kathy could fight her own battles.

As I drove to work, I gave myself a good talking to. I had to hang onto the positivity of the weekend. It was time to start looking on the bright side of life. No more negativity for me. I wasn't going to let anything drag me down.

"Good morning, Jill."

Spoke too soon.

"Mr Ivers? I thought you weren't working on the toll bridge anymore?"

"There's a bug going around. Very nasty from all accounts—lots of toilet activity."

Way too much information. "So, you had to step into the breach?"

"Precisely."

"It's not a permanent move, then?"

"No. I'm needed back at the office. They can't afford to lose me for any length of time."

I bet. "Well, I'd better get going." I handed over the toll fee.

"Did you enjoy the last issue of my newsletter? I thought there were some particularly good articles this time around."

"Your newsletter was invaluable this month. Anyway, got to rush. Bye."

I wasn't sure Mr Ivers would have appreciated it if he'd known that I'd used his newsletter to send me to sleep when I'd been to see Edward Hedgelog, holder of the dream-stone. I still had mixed feelings about my 'consultation' with Edward, but at least I hadn't had the nightmare since then.

***

"Jill!" Jules stood up from behind her desk as soon as I walked into the office. "Thank goodness you're back."

"What's the matter? It's not Winky, is it? Is he all right?"

"The cat's fine. Although, I don't know how you put up with him in your office all the time. He would drive me crazy."

"What is it, then?"

"It's Mrs V."

"Is she poorly?"

"No, yes, I don't know."

"Come on, Jules, spit it out! What's wrong?"

"She's been acting strangely."

"Mrs V is always strange."

"I know, but she's being even stranger than usual."

"In what way?"

"You know how we both agreed to come in while you were off for two days? She started being funny with me yesterday—ordering me around, and generally being really nasty."

"Maybe she was just feeling under the weather?"

"I don't think it was that. When I asked her why she wasn't knitting, she bit my head off. She said we didn't come to work to waste time knitting."

"She said what?" Now I really was worried. Mrs V lived to knit. "Okay, I'll have a word with her tomorrow. I'm sure it'll be okay. Anyway, how are things between you and Jethro?"

"It's over. I dumped him because he wouldn't quit the dance troupe."

"Maybe that was for the best. There's plenty more fish in the sea."

"Gilbert has contacted me."

"You mean Spotty?"

"Jill!" Jules gave me the sort of disapproving look that I normally got from Mrs V.

"Sorry. I didn't mean to say that, but isn't he the guy who was acne challenged?"

"Yes, but his skin is much better since he found a new formula cream."

"So you've seen him?"

"Not in person. He sent me a text with a photo attached." She took out her phone. "Look."

I was gobsmacked. The last time I'd seen Gilbert, his face had been covered in acne, but now he had a perfectly clear complexion. Whatever he was using certainly seemed to be doing the job.

"What will you do? Are you going to see him again?"

"I don't know. I told him I'd think about it."

I'd no sooner walked through to my office than Winky started on at me.

"She has to go! You have to sack her!"

"Who?"

"The old bag lady, of course. Who do you think?"

"I've told you a thousand times that I'm not getting rid of Mrs V."

"Yeah, but that was before."

"Before what?"

"Before she started throwing me around the office."

"Don't exaggerate."

"I'm not exaggerating. Yesterday, I was sitting over there minding my own business when she threw me straight across the room. I had to hide under the sofa. She's a psycho, that woman."

"I've already promised Jules that I'll have a word with Mrs V tomorrow."

"Those words had better be: 'You're fired'."

Winky huffed and puffed a little more, but then went back to the sofa where he picked up a book and began to read.

"More fishing books?"

"Nah, I got fed up of fly-fishing. Too much sitting around doing nothing for my liking."

"So, what's the book?" I walked over to the sofa. "Hypnosis for beginners?" I laughed.

"And what, may I ask, is so funny about that?"

"Hypnosis is not really a thing, is it? It's just a clever

stage act."

"Once again, you demonstrate how very little you know about anything. Hypnosis is very real, and in the right hands, can be a very powerful tool."

"If you say so. No one is ever going to convince me. I'd like to see someone try to hypnotise me."

"We'll see," he said, and then went back to his book. At least now that he'd given up on the fly fishing, I wouldn't have to worry about him snatching hats off people's heads.

A chill descended on the office, and I knew I was about to be visited by a ghost—I just didn't know which one.

"Colonel! Priscilla! How nice to see you both. How did the wedding go?"

The colonel and Priscilla had decided to do away with a long engagement, and had tied the knot. Circumstances had dictated that they'd had to marry in Ghost Town, which had meant I'd been unable to attend the ceremony. I'd been devastated, as you can imagine.

"It was a fabulous day," Priscilla said. "Wasn't it, Briggsy?"

"What? Oh, yes. Fabulous." The colonel seemed distracted.

"Are you okay, Colonel?"

"Not really. We've had some terrible news, haven't we, Cilla?"

Priscilla took the colonel's hand. "It'll be okay, Briggsy."

"I wish I shared your optimism."

"What's the problem?" I asked.

"It's the house." The colonel sighed. "It's going to be demolished."

"How come?"

"The new owners—those naked people—received an offer from a local property developer who wants to build twenty ugly houses on the site. That same man had contacted me numerous times when I was alive, but I'd always sent him packing. No amount of money could have persuaded me to part with my beautiful house. Unfortunately, it seems that the current owner is more interested in making a quick buck than in preserving my house."

"That's terrible. Has the sale gone through yet?"

"I don't think so, but it's only a matter of time. Cilla and I have been working overtime trying to scare away the property developer, but the man is too stupid to even notice our presence. I don't know what to do. I feel so helpless. I don't suppose there's anything you can do to help, is there, Jill?"

"I'm not sure there is. Unless there's something illegal going on, then it's hard to see what I can do."

"Would you at least do some checks on the man, just to see if there is a glimmer of hope?"

"Of course. Leave it with me."

With that, the colonel and Priscilla took their leave. I was sorry to see the colonel so unhappy, but even more so to learn the fate of his beautiful house.

Chapter 2

Winky had just fallen asleep on the sofa when the intercom buzzed. He jumped so much that he almost fell off.

"Jill." Jules' voice came through. "I have A Clowne for you. He doesn't have an appointment. Can you see him?"

"A clown?" I hated clowns with a passion. Evil, every last one of them.

"Yes. Mr Andrew Clowne."

"Oh, right, I see. Please show him in, Jules."

Mr Clowne was dressed in a charcoal suit. He had short, brown hair which was thinning on top.

"Thank you for seeing me, Miss Gooder."

"Call me Jill, please. Take a seat. Would you like a drink?"

"No, thanks. I'd prefer to get straight down to business, if you don't mind."

"Certainly. What is it I can do for you?"

"I'm a clown."

"Yes, so I understand. Andrew Clowne."

"No. I mean that I'm a clown."

Was it me? Or was this man being deliberately obtuse?

"I understand. Your name is Andrew Clowne."

"That's right. My name *is* Andrew Clowne, but I'm also a clown."

"Ah, now I see. It was a clever idea to change your name like that."

"Sorry? I don't follow."

"Changing your name to Andrew Clowne, so you could be: A Clowne, a clown."

"I didn't change my name. Andrew Clowne is my given

name."

My head was spinning. "What exactly is it I can do for you, Mr Clowne?"

"I'm the chairman of NOCA. Or at least I will be until after the annual conference which is to be held next week."

"Knocker? What's that?"

"N-O-C-A. It stands for the National Organisation of Clown Acts."

"Of course."

"The conference is to be held right here in Washbridge. Unfortunately, a very serious issue has arisen, which is why I'm here. Firstly, it's important I emphasise that discretion is essential."

"Jill Discretion Gooder - that's me. Discretion is my middle name."

To say he was supposed to be a clown, the man didn't have much of a sense of humour. I was feeding him my best material, and he was staring at me stony-faced.

"What is the 'serious issue' that has arisen, Mr Clowne?"

He looked furtively around the office, as though expecting to see someone hiding there.

"We have received a threatening letter, which said that if the conference goes ahead, there will be deaths."

"Do you mean they're threatening to kill someone at the conference?"

"Precisely. The letter says that two people will be murdered, unless we agree to pay them."

"They're demanding money?"

"Yes, and a lot of it. Thirty thousand pounds, to be precise."

"Surely, and I say this with the greatest of respect, an organisation such as yours could never come up with that kind of money?"

"NOCA has existed for a very long time, and every month each member is required to make a payment of ten pence, over and above their membership fee, into the organisation's contingency fund. Since its inception, that fund has never been needed, and currently stands at a little over sixty thousand pounds."

"Gosh! How many clowns are there in your organisation?"

"At any one time, there can be as many as five thousand, but only a very small percentage of those will be attending the conference."

"What exactly would you like me to do?"

"Find out who is behind the threat, and stop them."

"Have you taken this to the police?"

"No. The committee discussed it, but decided that it wouldn't be in our interest to do so. The publicity would be disastrous, and of course this could just be a hoax."

"Do you think that's likely?"

"I might have, had it not been for the murders."

"Murders?"

"Over the last twelve months two clowns have been murdered."

"I don't remember reading anything about that."

"That's hardly surprising. The murders were six months apart, and in different areas of the country. The victims were not high-profile clowns—just enthusiastic amateurs."

"I take it the murderer has never been caught?"

"No, but the threatening letter referred to the two

murders, and claimed that the writer had been responsible for them."

"I have to ask this. Have you considered paying these people off?"

"Certainly not. We will never give in to threats."

"Quite right. There isn't much to go on. Perhaps the first step would be for me to meet with the rest of your committee. Could that be arranged?"

"Yes, I can organise that. Will tomorrow be okay?"

"That'll be fine."

As soon as Mr Clowne had left, Winky jumped onto my desk.

"And that guy is supposed to be a clown?" Winky rolled his one eye. "He's about as funny as the bubonic plague. Anyway, I'm surprised that you agreed to take on the case."

"Why do you say that?"

"Because you're terrified of clowns."

"Don't be ridiculous. Of course I'm not."

I was already beginning to have second thoughts. What had I been thinking? A conference of clowns? That would make my 'corridors' nightmare seem like a sweet dream. I had to crack this case ahead of the conference. Under no circumstances did I want to put myself through that ordeal.

To take my mind off it, and because I was feeling a little peckish, I magicked myself over to Cuppy C. Since the twins had got rid of the ice maidens, and following on from the publicity which the Adrenaline Boys had generated, customer numbers were almost back to their previous level.

Amber and Pearl were behind the tea room counter.

"Hey, girls. Are you two scared of clowns?" I was studying the muffins. I fancied a change from blueberry, but couldn't quite decide between strawberry and Black Forest. Such were the crucial decisions I was called upon to make every day.

"Clowns?" Amber looked puzzled. "Why would anybody be scared of clowns? They're funny."

"Yeah." Pearl nodded. "They're my favourite part of the circus. Why do you ask?"

"I've just taken on a new case for an organisation of clowns."

"You're not scared of them, are you, Jill?" Amber said.

"Me? No, of course not. There's nothing to be scared of. At all. Not even a little bit."

"Have you made your mind up?" Pearl tapped the counter.

"About the clown case?"

"No. About which muffin you'd like."

"I think I'll go for the Black Forest."

"We'll soon have a whole new range of cakes for you to choose from," Amber said. "We're going to be buying from a new supplier. Their cakes are totally different to anything that's gone before. They call it 'Baking Reimagined'."

Oh dear! "What's that supposed to mean?"

"It's brand spanking new. We'll be the first tea room in Candlefield to have them."

I felt like I'd been down this road so many times before. Why was it that I was the only one who could see the juggernaut heading straight for us?

"You've had Mr Snake around here again, peddling his

oil, haven't you?"

"I know we've made a few mistakes in the past," Pearl conceded. "But this time, it's different."

"It always is. What exactly does Baking Reimagined mean?"

"Look at this." Amber handed me a leaflet: 'Baking Reimagined by Emperor Baking Enterprises'. "You'll be able to see for yourself. We'll be getting the first delivery in a few days. We'll be having a massive launch party to celebrate."

Sometimes it felt like all I ever did was pour cold water on the twins' ideas, so I decided to bite my tongue. Maybe this time everything would go according to plan.

What? I can dream, can't I?

"When do you give your talk at CASS?" Amber handed me the Black Forest muffin.

"At the end of the week. I'm beginning to wish I'd never agreed to do it."

"I'd hate to have to give a speech," Pearl said.

"It's not the speech I'm worried about. It's travelling on the airship that terrifies me. And then there are the dragons."

"Talking of dragons," Amber passed me the coffee. "I overheard Grandma saying something about dragons the other day."

"You were lucky she didn't turn you into a donkey," Pearl said. "If she'd known you were eavesdropping, you'd have been in real trouble."

"Why would Grandma be talking about dragons?" I asked.

"I don't know." Amber shrugged. "I only got to hear part of the conversation."

It was probably just as well that I didn't know. "How are you getting along with your new tenants?" I gestured upstairs.

The twins both frowned.

"Don't tell me that you're having problems with them already?"

"The guys are nice enough," Pearl said. "And at least we don't have to worry that they'll try to sabotage our business."

"So what's the problem, then?"

"You know how they're called the Adrenaline Boys?" Amber said. "Well, when they come back from one of their performances, they kind of live up to their name."

I must have looked puzzled because Amber continued. "The smell of sweaty socks is overpowering."

"So I was right." I laughed. "They really are the Sweaty Boys. What are you going to do about it?"

"Amber is going to have a word with them," Pearl said.

"No, I'm not. You are."

"Why should I do it?"

"You were the one who told them they could have the rooms."

"I did not. You did."

Oh boy! Time to change the subject, methinks.

"Has Daze gone away with Haze?"

"Yeah." Amber was still glaring at Pearl. "They left a couple of days ago."

"Can you believe it?" Pearl shook her head. "Daze has left Blaze in charge. What a nightmare!"

"I'm sure he'll be okay. Anyway, I think I'll go and see Aunt Lucy while I'm over here."

"I don't imagine you've heard about Lester, have you?"

Amber said.

"Heard what?"

"He's been suspended from his job."

"Why? What happened?"

"No idea. They won't tell us anything, as usual."

"I'd better go over there to find out what's happening."

Aunt Lucy and Lester were in the kitchen. Even if the twins hadn't forewarned me, I would have known that something was wrong because you could cut the atmosphere with a knife.

"Cup of tea, Jill?" Aunt Lucy offered.

"No, thanks. I've just been in Cuppy C. The twins said something about Lester being suspended."

At this, Lester looked up for the first time.

"That's right." He sighed. "It happened a few days ago."

"Why?"

"I was processing the paperwork for a client when I inadvertently checked the wrong box. I should have ticked the box which read 'via Ghost Town', but instead I ticked the one which read 'bypass Ghost Town'."

"Oh dear. Does that mean the client will be sent straight to—?"

"Exactly. It was a stupid mistake. That sort of thing is Grim Reaper 101. I can only put it down to being distracted."

He glanced at Aunt Lucy, and I saw her give an almost imperceptible shake of the head. And then the penny dropped.

"Oh no. Did this happen when I saw you in the street close to my office?"

He hesitated.

"Lester!" I pressed. "Tell me. Was it seeing me there that put you off?"

"I told you not to say anything, Lester," Aunt Lucy said.

"I feel terrible." I joined him at the table. "Can't I just tell them that it was my fault?"

"It wasn't your fault, Jill," he said. "I shouldn't have allowed myself to be so easily distracted."

"So what's going to happen?"

"I have to wait to hear back from them as to what course of action they'll take."

"But you'll still be able to carry on with the training?"

"I don't know. I just don't know."

Chapter 3

I said my goodbyes to Aunt Lucy and Lester, and then magicked myself back to Washbridge. I still felt dreadful that I was the one responsible for Lester being suspended from his job. I had to think of a way to put things right, and it occurred to me that maybe Mad could help. I gave her a call.

"I've got a bit of a problem, Mad. I'm hoping you might be able to help."

"I will if I can. Anything to take my mind off Mum's stupid wedding."

"You remember Lester, don't you?"

"Of course."

"He's recently started training in a new job. He signed up to become a grim reaper."

"Really? I know my job is a little strange, but I could never do that. What does your Aunt Lucy think about it?"

"She hates the whole thing, but that's not the problem. He's been undergoing training with a more experienced operative, and the other day I happened to stumble across him while he was attending to one of his—err—clients. I must've distracted him because he filled in the form incorrectly. He should have ticked the box which said 'via Ghost Town', but instead ticked the box which said 'bypass Ghost Town'."

"Oh dear. That's not good."

"I know. That's why they've suspended him. It's all my fault. If I hadn't been there, he probably wouldn't have made the error. I have to put this right, but I don't know how. I thought I'd talk to you to see if you had any bright ideas."

"How long ago was this?"

"Only a few days."

"There have been some delays with all the transport systems recently, so maybe there's still time to do something about it. Do you have his—err—client's details?"

"No, but I know when and where the incident took place."

"That should be enough. Send me that information by text, and I'll see what I can do, but I wouldn't want you to get your hopes up."

***

Before going home, I decided to call into the office, just in case there were any messages waiting for me. As soon as I walked in, Jules began to speak, but not to me. She was talking to her computer screen. Perhaps she was on Skype? I didn't want to interrupt, so I tiptoed over to my office.

Winky was standing on the sofa, looking at the mirror on the wall. He appeared to be talking to his own reflection. What was the matter with everyone in this office? I was beginning to think I was the only sane person there.

"Winky? What are you doing?"

"What does it look like?"

"It looks like you're talking to your reflection."

"I'm practising my hypnosis."

"Why would you try to hypnotise yourself?"

"I don't have any other subjects, unless you're volunteering?"

"No chance."

"Why not? If you're so sure it doesn't work, then what are you afraid of?"

"I'm not afraid of anything. I've just got better things to do with my time than to indulge your weird obsessions."

"In that case, you'd better allow me to carry on with my practice."

"Knock yourself out."

I tried to ignore Winky, and focus on checking the day's post which mostly comprised of bills, two of which were red.

"Jill, do you have a minute?" Jules had popped her head around the door.

"Sure, take a seat."

She looked rather guilty, and it took her a few minutes to gather the courage to speak.

"You're probably wondering what I was doing when you came in just now."

"I was a little surprised to see you talking to your computer."

"I won't let it interfere with my work."

"Won't let *what* interfere with your work?"

"I've started my own YouTube channel. It's called 'Young Knits'. There are lots of channels for older, more experienced knitters, but very few for young people. I thought it might be fun to show others what I've learned."

"How long have you been doing it?"

"I started a few days ago; I've only got three subscribers up to now. But like I said, I won't let it interfere with my work here. I'll only make a recording when I have no other work to do."

"What about if we get a visitor while you're recording

your piece?"

"I won't be doing it very often, probably only once a week. If a visitor arrives while I'm recording, I'll obviously stop. So, is it okay?"

"I suppose so."

"You can subscribe to my channel if you like, Jill."

"Yeah, maybe I will." *The same day as I join the clown appreciation society.*

Jules looked over at Winky who was walking around and around in circles. "What's the matter with the cat?"

"He's all right. You'd better get back to work."

"Okay. Thanks again for being so understanding."

I waited until she was out of the office, and then walked over to the crazy cat.

"Winky! Winky!"

He didn't react at all. He just continued to walk around and around in circles.

"Winky?" I snapped my fingers next to his ear. "Winky, wake up!"

He stopped walking and shook his head. "Did it work?"

"Did what work?"

"I hypnotised myself."

"I'm not falling for that. You were just putting it on."

"No, I wasn't. So it did work then?"

"I'm not playing your silly games, Winky."

What kind of fool did he take me for?

I decided to call it a day, and threw the bills into the bottom drawer.

"Just because you can't see them." Winky jumped onto my desk. "Doesn't mean you don't have to pay them."

"Let me worry about my finances, would you?"

"If you get thrown out on the street, so do I. Why don't you let me help?"

"I don't need financial advice from a cat, and particularly not from one who believes in hypnosis."

"Look into my eyes." He began to move his paw slowly from side-to-side in front of my face. "Look deeply into my eyes."

"Don't be ridiculous!"

"You are becoming drowsy. Your eyelids are heavy." His voice seemed to echo around my head.

I didn't have any more time for his nonsense. "Get off my desk!"

***

As soon as I got out of the car, Mrs Rollo called me over. Even before I got to her door, I could see that she was upset about something.

"Whatever's the matter, Mrs Rollo?"

"Come in, would you, Jill?" She was close to tears.

I followed her into the kitchen where it took her a few minutes to compose herself.

"I don't know what to do, Jill. I've been so stupid."

"Sit down, Mrs Rollo. Let me make us both a cup of tea, and then you can tell me all about it."

"Okay. That's very kind of you. There are some buns in the cupboard if you'd like one?"

"No, it's okay. I don't want to spoil my dinner."

I made tea for the two of us, and then joined her at the kitchen table.

"What's happened, Mrs Rollo?"

"I had a man come to the door a few days ago. He asked

if I enjoyed going away on holidays. I said I did. He said that his company was offering life-time timeshare holidays in Spain. I told him that I could never afford anything like that, but he said these were much less expensive than usual. Just a one-off one-thousand-pound fee. He showed me the brochure. The accommodation was magnificent, located almost on the beach. I thought it would be ideal for me, Sheila and her husband, and of course, Justin."

"Did you sign anything?"

"It's worse than that. I gave him cash."

"How much?"

"The full amount. He said that he would come back again the next morning with all the paperwork, but he never showed up."

"Maybe he's ill? Or got his appointments mixed up?"

"That's what I thought at first, but when I tried to ring the number on his card, it was unrecognised. I'm not even sure the company exists. That money is from my savings." She dabbed her eyes with a tissue. "Whatever shall I do?"

"Do you still have his card?"

"Yes." She stood up, walked over to the drawer, and took out a leaflet and a business card. "This is what he left me."

"What did he look like?"

"I'd say he was in his late fifties, and was practically bald. And he smelled of meat."

"Meat?"

"I think it was meat. Maybe it was just his aftershave. He was very charming though."

They always are.

"Try not to worry about it, Mrs Rollo. I'll do some

digging around, and see what I can find out."

"Do you think I'll get my money back?"

"I can't promise, but I'll certainly do my best for you."

By the time I left Mrs Rollo's house, I was seething with anger. I hated people who preyed on the vulnerable in that way. If I got my hands on him, he'd be sorry.

***

I'd no sooner got into the house than there was a knock at the door. Perhaps Mrs Rollo had remembered more information about the conman.

"I have another letter for you." It was the same Candlefield Special Delivery man who had brought the invitation from CASS.

"Oh? Hello again. It's Laurence, isn't it?"

"Please call me Puddles. Everyone does." He handed me an envelope which bore the CASS watermark.

"Thanks, Puddles. Isn't it rather late to be delivering letters?"

"Not at all. CSD delivers at all times of the day and night. Anyway, I'd better run. This is my last delivery of the day, and Mrs Puddles will have my dinner ready in a few minutes."

Back inside, I ripped open the envelope. Inside was a return ticket for the journey on the CASS airship. My nerves began to jangle again. I wasn't very good on an aeroplane, so I dreaded to think how I'd feel on board an airship.

Jack's car pulled onto the drive, so I quickly slipped the envelope and ticket into my bag. I couldn't imagine how I would ever explain that away.

"Hello, beautiful." Jack greeted me with a smile.

"Don't think you can butter me up like that."

"What did I do this time?" He hung up his coat.

"You told Kathy that we'd have the kids tomorrow night."

"So? You love those kids."

"I love them in small doses, and at a distance. What possessed you to suggest we have them over here?"

"I thought it would be an adventure for them."

"Can you imagine what kind of mess they're going to make?"

"Mrs Mopp is due to come the following day, so it doesn't matter. And besides, it will be nice to have the kids here. It'll be fun."

"You've never looked after young kids, have you, Jack?"

"No, but how difficult can it be?"

Men? Clueless. Every last one of them.

Jack had made dinner, so it was my turn to do the washing up. The sooner we bought a dishwasher, the better.

"Have you looked at this, Jill?" Jack was sitting at the kitchen table.

"What is it?"

"The wedding gift list for Deli and Nails' wedding?"

"Not yet." I'd deliberately ignored it ever since Mad had dropped it off.

"There are some very strange things on here." He flicked through the pages.

"Such as?"

"All of the gift lists I've ever seen have included things

like toasters, wine racks, cutlery, and that sort of thing. This one has an electric toenail clipper, and a home tanning studio."

"I did warn you about this wedding. We should have declined the invitation like I wanted to. You've got a rude awakening coming."

"I'm sure you're exaggerating, Jill. You usually do. So? What do you think? The toenail clipper or the home tanning studio?"

Chapter 4

Thank goodness Mr Ivers wasn't on duty at the toll bridge the next morning. I don't think I could have handled another dose of Ivy. I was half way to work when I realised that I needed to call in and buy salmon for Winky. Five tins ought to be enough.

I'd just parked the car when my phone rang.

"Jill, I just wanted to check that Jack is still coming around to pick the kids up tonight?"

"Morning to you too, Kathy. Yes, I'm okay, thanks for asking."

"Sorry. I'm just excited about the show tonight. I don't want anything to spoil it. You and Jack are still okay to have the kids, aren't you?"

"Yes. Jack can't wait."

"What about you?"

"I'm counting the minutes. Are they going to bring some toys with them?"

"We bought some retro board games at the weekend. We thought it would be a good idea for them to bring those. That way you and Jack can play with them."

"Retro board games?"

"You know—Snakes and Ladders, Ludo, that kind of thing."

"Why would anyone want to play those? They're boring."

"You only think they're boring because you lost every time we played when you were a kid."

"I did not lose every time."

"The only time you didn't lose was when you cheated."

"I've never cheated at board games."

"You have a selective memory, Jill. Can't you remember when Dad sent you to bed early because you'd been sneaking money out of the Monopoly box?"

"I was framed."

"If you say so. I'll see you tonight, then."

***

When I walked into the office, Mrs V glanced up, but didn't speak. Instead, she went back to her typing. Her desk looked different, and it took me a few moments to realise why. There were no knitting needles or crochet hooks, or even balls of wool to be seen.

"Morning, Mrs V. How are you?"

"Good morning. Very well, thank you," she said, without once looking up from the computer screen.

"Why aren't you knitting today, Mrs V?"

"I'm rather too busy for knitting."

Jules had been right. Mrs V wasn't herself at all. Too busy to knit? Something was definitely amiss.

Winky was reading his hypnosis book, but put it down when I walked into my office.

"She's been at it again," he said. "The old bag lady was in here earlier, rifling through your drawers."

"Are you sure?"

"I suppose it could have been a kangaroo. Of course, I'm sure. She's acting really weird, that one."

He was right. Mrs V wasn't herself, and I needed to find out why. But first, I had to give Winky his salmon and cream.

"There you go, boy."

"How very kind. You really shouldn't have."

For the rest of the morning, Winky had a stupid, self-satisfied smirk on his face, but I couldn't work out why. He was definitely up to something. I would have to keep my wits about me.

I needed coffee, but with Mrs V being in the mood she was, I didn't like to ask her to make it. And anyway, a bit of fresh air would be good for me. I walked down the high street to Coffee Triangle. I'd checked beforehand—it was tambourine day, so the noise levels shouldn't be too off-putting. Outside Ever A Wool Moment, there was a crowd of people, staring and pointing at the window. What marketing promotion had Grandma come up with this time?

I managed to push my way through to the front of the crowd, and could now see what all the fuss was about. Grandma had once again surpassed herself. The window display had been turned over to a promotion for Dragon Wool, which according to the blurb was a unique range of colours never seen before. But it wasn't the wool which was attracting everyone's attention. All eyes were on the glass cage inside the shop window. Inside that cage was a small dragon.

"I've never seen such a realistic animated figure before," the woman standing next to me said.

"It's so cute," her companion said.

I wouldn't have called it cute. It was true that it was quite tiny, but it had sharp claws, and a mouthful of even sharper teeth. Several people commented on how realistic it was, and they were right. I had a horrible feeling the reason it looked so realistic was because it was a real dragon. That would explain why Amber had overheard

Grandma talking about dragons. The woman was unbelievable. It was bad enough that she openly flaunted her magical powers in the human world, but it seemed that she had now imported a dragon as well.

Just as I'd expected, Coffee Triangle was very quiet. There were no more than a dozen people in there, and only a few of those were shaking tambourines. I'd only intended to have a drink, but the strawberry cupcakes called to me, so what could I do? It would have been rude to ignore them.

I'd just taken a big bite of cupcake when I heard a familiar voice.

"Jill, do you mind if I join you?" It was Hilary from Love Spell.

I couldn't speak because my mouth was full of delicious strawberryness, so I gestured for her to take the seat opposite me.

"Sorry about that," I said, once I'd managed to swallow the cake. "How are you?"

"Very well, thanks. How about you and Jack?"

"We're doing great, thanks. Mind you, I'm not very happy with him this morning because he's volunteered us to babysit my sister's kids tonight."

"You'll enjoy it. And besides, it will be good practice for you two. I assume you'll be starting a family soon?"

It was just as well I didn't still have a mouthful of cupcake, or I might have spit it out.

"We've only just got our own place. There'll be plenty of time for kids later."

"That's what they all say."

It was time to change the subject. "How's the dating business?"

"Business is booming at the moment. More witches than ever seem to want to move to the human world."

"It's funny you should say that because I'm actually giving a talk at Candlefield Academy of Supernatural Studies later this week. The headmistress wants me to point out to the pupils that not everything about the human world is rosy. She's concerned about the large number of young sups who seem intent on moving here."

"You're going to CASS? I'm jealous. When I was a kid, I really wanted to go there, but I never got an invitation. Even now, I'd love to see the place. I assume that you'll be going on the airship?"

"Don't remind me. I'm dreading it."

"Why? It'll be amazing. And then there are the dragons."

"I'm trying not to think about those. Anyway, I'm glad to hear your business is doing well."

"It is. There's only one fly in the ointment. We're having a little bit of trouble with our new neighbours. They moved into the building a few months ago, and ever since then they've been pestering us to vacate our office so that they can move into it. We've told them that we don't want to move, and that we're happy where we are, but they won't take no for an answer."

"You should tell them to 'do one'."

"Normally, I would, but they're lawyers, and I don't want to end up in court."

"This firm of lawyers? They aren't by any chance called Armitage, Armitage, Armitage and Poole, are they?"

"How ever did you guess?"

Before she left, I gave Hilary a few tips on how to deal with Gordon Armitage.

Hilary and I had been talking for so long that it wasn't worth going back to the office because I had an appointment with the NOCA committee. We'd arranged to meet at their offices which appropriately enough were located in Chuckle House.

The receptionist seemed out of place because she looked as though she'd just spent the last half-hour sucking on a lemon.

"Yes?" She didn't even try to hide her boredom.

"I'm here to meet with the NOCA committee. My name is—"

"Doesn't matter. It's that door over there." She pointed.

"Don't you need me to sign in or anything?"

"Doesn't matter. You can go straight in."

Despite her instructions, I felt I should at least knock on the door.

"Come in." I recognised Andrew Clowne's voice.

Seated at a round table was the aforementioned Andrew Clowne and two other men. "Do have a seat, Ms Gooder. This is Mr Ray Carter." He pointed to the man seated to his right. He too was miserable. The only funny thing about him was his hair which he'd obviously tried to dye black, but which had turned out several shades of grey. "And this is Mr Donald Keigh."

Don Keigh? Before I could stop myself, I laughed. "Is that a stage name?"

All three of them looked puzzled. None more so than Donald Keigh.

"Sorry?" he said.

"I just assumed that Donald Keigh must be a stage name."

"No. Why would you think that?"

"No reason. Never mind."

"I went to see Ms Gooder at her office, yesterday," Andrew Clowne said. "I've brought her up to speed with our little problem. She wanted to talk to all of us together, which is why I've asked her here today. So, over to you, Ms Gooder."

"Thank you, Mr Clowne." I somehow managed to stifle a laugh. "Is it okay if I call you Andrew?"

"I suppose that will be all right."

"I wanted to speak to all of you, so I could get your thoughts on the 'problem'. Specifically, I'd like to know why you don't want to take this to the police."

"*I* do want to take it to the police," Ray Carter said. "But I was outvoted."

"Involving the police would be a mistake," Donald Keigh said. "There's a good chance that this is all a hoax, but if we bring in the police, then we can kiss goodbye to this year's conference. Do you think they'll let us go ahead with it if we tell them about the threats that have been made?"

"We can't allow this to get out to the press," Carter said. "It would be disastrous. Attendances have been down year-on-year for the last six years. If this was to be made public, then they would fall even more. We simply can't afford for that to happen."

"There isn't much time for me to track down the extortionist ahead of the conference," I said. "What's your plan if I'm unable to do that?"

"The conference will go ahead anyway." Andrew Clowne got in before the others could speak.

"Is that a good idea?" I asked.

"Cancelling the conference isn't an option," Donald Keigh insisted.

"That's right." Andrew Clowne nodded. "If you haven't managed to catch the man before then, we'll need you to go undercover on the day."

"When you say 'undercover', what exactly do you mean?"

"You'll have to attend the conference dressed as a clown, obviously."

Dress as a clown? Me? That was all my worst nightmares rolled into one. I would have to solve this case before the day of the conference. Failure wasn't an option.

"Do you have the letter with the extortion demands?"

Andrew Clowne opened his briefcase, took out the letter, and passed it to me. It had been produced by cutting words out of newspapers, and gluing them to the page. Unless thirty thousand pounds was handed over, two people would be killed during the upcoming conference. The extortionist said he had killed and wouldn't hesitate to kill again. The committee had been instructed to confirm their willingness to pay the money by placing a short ad in the classified section of Clown Weekly magazine.

"What do you think we should do about the ad?" Ray Carter asked.

"Nothing. Let's see what happens when he realises that you're not going to play ball. With a bit of luck, calling his bluff may scare him off."

We talked for another forty-five minutes, and all three men agreed to make themselves available for questioning if and when I needed them.

Chapter 5

I was still concerned about Mrs V, so as I was already in that part of town, I decided to drop in on Armi to see if he'd also noticed a change in her. Armitage, Armitage, Armitage and Poole had relocated across town, and now shared a building with Love Spell.

The young woman on reception ignored me until she had finished checking messages on her phone.

"Good morning," she eventually managed. "Welcome to Armitage, Armitage, Armitage and Poole. How can I help you?"

Before I could reply, a familiar, but unwelcome voice interrupted us.

"What are you doing here?" Gordon Armitage was just as ugly as ever.

"Morning to you too, Gordon. Winky sends his love. How are you keeping?"

"I asked why you were here?"

"I'm keeping very well, thank you, Gordon. Nice of you to ask."

"Still the smartass, I see. If you don't have any business here, I must ask you to leave."

"I'm here to see Armi."

"About what?"

"I don't think that's any of your business."

"You're in my offices; that makes it my business."

"Speaking of offices, I hear you're up to your old tricks again."

"What are you talking about now?"

"What is it with you, Gordon? Why do you feel the need to expand your empire at the expense of others?"

"You're talking in riddles."

"I hear that you're trying to drive someone out of their offices in the same way as you did with me."

"Who did you hear that from?"

"Is it true?"

"It has nothing whatsoever to do with you. Now, if there's nothing else, I'd like you to leave or I'll be forced to call security."

"I wonder if the newspapers would be interested in the story of a firm of solicitors who take pleasure in driving out innocent businesses simply to extend their own premises? I doubt that would reflect well on Armitage, Armitage, Armitage and Poole."

"Is that a threat?"

"More of a promise. I strongly recommend that you leave Love Spell alone. And now, if you wouldn't mind, I'd like to see Armi, please."

Gordon Armitage hesitated for a moment, but then stormed off. The receptionist, who had been transfixed by the confrontation, made a call to Armi.

"Jill? What are you doing here?" Armi appeared from a door on my right. "Is Annabel alright?"

"I was going to ask you exactly the same thing. Have you seen her recently?"

"Not for a couple of days. I've tried calling her, but she hasn't picked up. And she didn't return my messages. Hasn't she been at work?"

"Yes, she's there now, but she's been acting rather strangely. That's why I thought I'd better come and see if you had any idea what was going on."

"I don't, I'm afraid."

"Not to worry. I'll have a chat with her when I get back

to the office, and try to get to the bottom of it."

**

Armi had confirmed my suspicions; something was amiss with Mrs V. It was as if she was hiding something. Perhaps she was ill, or maybe she was having problems with her sister again. Whatever it was, I intended to get to the bottom of it.

She wasn't at her desk when I got back, but I could hear movement from inside my office. It sounded as though someone was throwing things around. I wasn't in the mood for Winky and his stupid games, and was all set to give him a piece of my mind.

"Winky! What do you think you're—"

It took me a few moments to register exactly what I was seeing. One thing was for sure—the culprit wasn't Winky. He was on the sofa, bound hand and foot, with a gag over his mouth. Mrs V had pulled out all the drawers of my desk; the contents were scattered across the floor. At that moment, it became clear that despite appearances, the person standing in front of me was not Mrs V.

"Who are you?" I shouted.

The 'doppelgänger' spell was obviously in play here. I closed my eyes, and focused, and then cast a spell which would reveal the person behind the 'mask'.

"Alicia!"

She grinned that evil grin of hers. Suddenly, the room was filled with a thick purple smoke. I could hardly see my hand in front of me, and had to feel my way over to the window by touch. As I did, I heard the outer door slam closed. Once I'd managed to open the window, the smoke slowly began to clear. Alicia was nowhere to be seen, so I hurried over to the sofa, and pulled the gag off Winky's mouth.

"Ouch!"

"Are you okay?"

"Yeah. Just untie me."

Five minutes later, Winky was free of his bonds, and we were sitting side by side on the sofa.

"What happened?" I said.

"She came in here and started to go through your desk. I realised it wasn't the old bag lady, so I jumped onto her back, and gave her a good clawing. But the next thing I knew, she had me trussed up like a turkey. Who was that, anyway?"

"That was an old *friend* of mine; her name is Alicia. She's an evil witch, but I can't for the life of me think what she could have been looking for. There's nothing in this office that would interest her."

"She needs teaching a lesson."

"Don't worry. I don't intend to let her get away with this, but first, I'd better get over to Mrs V's house to see if she's okay."

It was a long time since I'd been to Mrs V's house. Fortunately, she'd given me a key some time ago in case of emergency. I knocked first, but there was no reply. If Alicia had hurt Mrs V in any way, I'd make sure she'd regret it for the rest of her life.

I let myself in, and called Mrs V's name. There was still no reply. I checked all the rooms downstairs, but there was no sign of her. I made my way slowly upstairs—terrified at what I might find. The bedroom door was slightly ajar, so I eased it open. Mrs V was lying on the bed; her eyes were closed. For a moment, I feared the worst, but when I checked her pulse, it was strong.

"Mrs V! Wake up! Mrs V!"

She didn't stir at all.

This wasn't normal sleep. She was under a strong 'sleep' spell which took all my focus to reverse. This was obviously the work of a very powerful witch; my money was on Ma Chivers.

"Jill? What are you doing here?" Mrs V sat up. "What time is it? Am I late for work?"

"I think you must have been poorly, Mrs V. You've been asleep for a couple of days."

"What? Really? Oh dear. The last thing I remember I was getting ready to go to work, but then someone came to the door."

"Do you remember who it was?"

"No, sorry. I can't remember a thing after opening the door. I suppose we'd better get a move on."

"Stay where you are." I put my hand on her shoulder. "There's no need for you to come in today. You need to rest up for a while until you're feeling better."

"Okay. I guess you're right. I do feel a little lightheaded."

I made Mrs V a cup of tea, and took her some biscuits. Only when I was sure she was okay, did I leave.

***

I should have known better than to think I'd seen the back of Alicia and Ma Chivers. Even though I'd racked my brain, I couldn't think what Alicia had been looking for in my office. There was nothing to find there.

Jack had finished work early, and was picking up the kids from Kathy's. I'd said I'd go straight home, and organise dinner for us all. I may have forgotten to mention to Jack that dinner would be takeaway pizza.

What? All kids love pizza, don't they?

"Hey, Jill." Blake called from across the street, and then came over to join me. "You're home early, aren't you?"

"I've got my sister's kids coming over tonight. We're babysitting while she and her husband go and see some pop star at Washbridge Arena."

"Murray Murray?"

"Yeah? How did you know?"

"We tried to get tickets, but they'd already sold out."

"I've never heard of him."

"You must be the only person in Washbridge who hasn't. I bet you're looking forward to having the kids over, aren't you?"

"Oh yeah." I lied. "How is Jen?"

"Great, thanks. Things have been so much better between us since I told her about you know what. We had a long talk about the importance of keeping it a secret. I thought we needed to, after what happened when Jack and I went bowling."

"And do you think she's got the message now?"

"Yeah. Everything's cool now. By the way, have you seen that someone is moving in next door to us?"

"I hadn't realised that the house was for sale."

"That's not surprising. It was sold before they even had a chance to put the 'for sale' board up."

"Have you met your new neighbours yet?"

"No. The only reason I know it's been sold is because I spoke to our old neighbours before they moved out. They were quite chuffed to have made such a quick sale. Anyway, I'd better get going. Have a good evening with the kids."

***

"Auntie Jill!" Lizzie came rushing into the kitchen.

"Auntie Jill!" Mikey was a couple of steps behind her.

"Hi, kids. You've got crisps?" There was a trail of crumbs behind them.

"Take your coats off, kids." Jack appeared in the doorway.

"You bought them crisps?" I gave him a look.

"They said they were hungry, so we stopped off at the minimarket."

"What about their dinner?"

"I knew it would be some time before you had it ready, so I thought the crisps would keep them going."

"I can't see any point in my slaving over a hot oven now the kids are full of crisps. I guess I'll just order takeaway. And I was so looking forward to cooking a proper dinner. Oh, well."

Jack eyed me suspiciously. He was onto my ruse.

"Do you have any toys, Auntie Jill?" Lizzie asked.

"No. Your mummy said that you were going to bring some with you?"

"They have," Jack said. "I've left them in the car. I'll just nip out and get them."

A few minutes later, Jack was back with a couple of board games, and something I hoped I'd never see again.

Lizzie grabbed the Frankensteinesque beanie from him.

"This one is my favourite." Lizzie held it out to me—I backed away. "It's a pandoceros. Can you guess which animals it's made from?"

"At a wild guess, could it be a panda and a rhinoceros?"

"How did you know?"

"Something about the name gave it away."

Mikey had finished his bag of crisps, and had dropped the empty packet onto the floor.

"Pick that up, Mikey, please."

"Will you show us some more magic tricks, Auntie Jill?" He had ignored my request to pick up the crisp packet.

"Auntie Jill doesn't know any magic," Jack said.

"Yes she does." Mikey was still ignoring the litter situation. "She showed us a magic trick once before, didn't you, Auntie Jill?"

"Yes, but that was the only trick that I know. Now, why don't you three set up one of the board games while I order the food?"

Chapter 6

I went through to the kitchen so I could hear myself think, but before I had the chance to order the pizza, I felt a chill in the room, and knew immediately that a ghost was about to appear.

"That man is driving me insane!" My mother was standing beside the kitchen table.

"Mum? What are you doing here?"

"Jill?" Jack's voice came from the other room. "Did you shout?"

"No. It's okay. I just dropped something." And then in a whisper, I said to my mother, "Mum, this isn't a good time. I've got my sister's kids in the other room. Can't we talk about this another day?"

"Your father is painting the front of his house red."

"So?"

"Didn't you hear what I just said? He's painting it red. It will bring down the tone of the whole neighbourhood."

Just then, the kitchen door opened, and in walked Lizzie.

"Who are you talking to, Auntie Jill?"

"No one. I was just talking to myself."

"Who's that lady?"

I glanced at my mother. Thankfully, she took the hint and disappeared.

"What lady?" I said.

"The lady dressed all in white. The one you were talking to. Where has she gone?"

What was going on? How had Lizzie seen my mother's ghost? Could she be a parahuman?

"I think you must have imagined it, Lizzie."

"I didn't. She was standing over there, but then she disappeared. Is she a ghost?"

"Ghost? No. There are no such things as ghosts."

"Yes, there are. There's one at our school. Her name is Caroline."

"Who's Caroline?"

"I told you. She's a ghost."

"Have you seen Caroline?"

"Yes. I often see her. In the main hall."

"Is she a lady?"

"No. She's a girl—like me."

"Has anyone else seen her?"

"I don't think so."

"Did you tell one of the teachers?"

"Yes. I told Miss Brakes, but she said there are no such things as ghosts."

"Did you tell your mummy or daddy?"

"I told Mummy, but she said I was being silly."

"It might be better not to mention the lady in white to them."

"Okay. Can I have a drink of pop please?"

***

'One Minute Takeaway' lived up to their name yet again; the pizza was at the door almost as soon as I'd finished placing the order. The kids and Jack had wanted to eat in the lounge while playing board games. No chance! I could only imagine what kind of devastation that would cause. Instead, I insisted that they come through to the kitchen where the four of us could eat at the table.

Fortunately, Lizzie didn't mention the woman in white again. Maybe she would just forget all about it.

"Can we play the board games now?" Mikey said. His face was covered in pizza.

"When I've cleaned you both up."

After I'd wiped the kids' faces and hands, they rushed off. Jack stood up, and was about to follow them.

"Hold your horses, mister. Where do you think you're going?"

"I thought we'd do the dishes later?" He looked confused.

"I wasn't talking about the dishes. Come here."

I took his hands and wiped them with the flannel. Then I wiped his mouth. "You're as bad as the kids."

"I want to play Ludo," Mikey said.

"No." Lizzie stamped her foot. "Ludo is boring. I want to play Snakes and Ladders."

"Ludo!"

"Snakes and Ladders!"

"Hold on there, kids," Jack said. "This is what we'll do. I'll toss this coin, and whichever one of you calls correctly, can decide which game we play first. Okay?"

The kids nodded in agreement.

"Mikey, call." Jack tossed the coin into the air.

"Heads."

"It's tails. Lizzie gets to choose which game we play first."

Mikey frowned, but didn't argue with the result. Since when had Jack been such an expert with kids?

I'd forgotten just how tedious Snakes and Ladders could be. And it wasn't just me who thought so. After thirty minutes, the kids had grown tired of it, and moved to the sofa to watch TV. It was a kids' program I'd never seen before, and it was incredibly noisy.

I made to stand up, but Jack caught hold of my arm. "Let's finish the game."

I knew why he'd said it. He was in the lead, and he sensed the opportunity to beat me at something.

"It's boring, Jack."

"If you're afraid of losing, you can always concede."

Concede? I never conceded. "No. We'll keep on playing."

Twenty minutes later, there were only five squares between him and victory.

Now, it's not that I'm a bad loser, I'm just a much better winner. He rolled the dice and got a three which should have taken him clear of the final snake. I quickly cast a spell which caused that snake to move one position to the left, which meant that Jack landed smack bang on top of it.

Snigger.

He stared at the board in disbelief. "That snake wasn't on that square."

"What do you mean?" I said, all innocent-like. "Are you suggesting it moved?"

"No—I—err."

"Are you going to move your piece or not?"

He slid it onto the square which now contained the snake. I leaned over, took hold of it, and slid it down the snake to the bottom of the board.

"Unlucky." I smirked. "And you were so close to winning."

Ten minutes later, I slid my piece onto the winning square.

"I win! Again!"

What? I did it for his own good. I didn't want him to get big-headed.

***

We tried to get the kids to play Ludo, but they were much more interested in watching TV. Jack, on the other hand, was determined to beat me at something. Unfortunately for him, he lost at that too. And no, I didn't cheat. Much.

It was almost eleven o'clock when Kathy and Peter arrived back from the show. Jack and I went out into the hallway to greet them. We didn't want to wake the kids who were both fast asleep. Lizzie was in the armchair; Mikey was stretched out on the sofa.

"How are the kids?" Kathy said, as soon as she walked through the door.

"They're both fine. They're asleep in the lounge."

"Have they been good?" Peter asked.

"Good as gold," Jack said. "They've been watching TV for most of the evening. I think the board games were too boring for them."

"Are you sure it wasn't because Jill wouldn't let them win?" Kathy grinned.

"What do you mean?"

"You never could bear to lose at any game. When we were kids, you always used to sulk if you lost."

"I did not sulk."

"If you say so."

"How was the concert?" Jack changed the subject.

"It was fantastic!" Kathy gushed. "Murray Murray was

great, wasn't he, Pete?"

"Yeah, he was really good."

"Mummy! Daddy!" Lizzie appeared in the doorway. "I thought I heard you. Did you have a nice time?"

"Yes, pumpkin, we had a really nice time. Did you enjoy yourself?"

"Auntie Jill doesn't have any toys. And she wouldn't show us any magic tricks."

"I don't know any more tricks, Lizzie."

"She does have a ghost, though, Mummy."

Kathy, Peter and Jack all looked at me. I shrugged.

"What do you mean, Lizzie?" Kathy said.

"There was a lady in Auntie Jill's kitchen. She was dressed in white. Auntie Jill was talking to her."

"Jill?" Kathy looked to me for an answer. I shrugged again, and beckoned for her to follow me into the kitchen. "What was that all about?" she asked, once I'd closed the kitchen door.

"I have no idea. They've both been asleep. Maybe Lizzie was having a dream about ghosts?"

"I guess that must be it. Anyway, thanks for having the kids. We had a great time. I'd love to meet Murray Murray in person. He seems like such a great guy."

When we went back into the hall, Mikey was standing next to his dad.

"Can we?" Mikey looked up with big sad eyes. "Please, Daddy?"

"You'll have to ask your mum." Peter passed the buck.

"Ask Mummy what?" Kathy said.

"Can we go and see the dragon, Mummy? Everyone from school has seen it already."

"Yes, Mummy!" Lizzie said. "Katie said it's really cute."

I gave Kathy a puzzled look.

"They're talking about that new promotional display that your grandmother has set up in the window of Ever."

"Do you know where she got it from?"

"Beats me." Kathy shrugged. "It wasn't there when I left in the evening, but then the next morning, there it was. I asked your grandmother where she'd got it from, but she never gave me an answer."

"Please, Mummy, can we go to see the dragon?" Mikey pulled at Kathy's skirt.

"Yes, I suppose so. Seeing as you've been good for Auntie Jill, I'll take you to see it tomorrow after school."

"Yes!" Mikey jumped for joy.

"Thanks, Mummy!" Lizzie beamed.

***

"That was great, wasn't it?" Jack said, as we settled down on the sofa with a glass of wine.

"The board games? Yeah, I really enjoyed those."

"Not the board games. I meant having Mikey and Lizzie around here. It's nice having kids in the house, don't you think?"

I took a long drink of wine. "They're okay in small doses, I suppose. Very small doses."

"They bring the house to life."

"The house is already alive enough for me, thank you very much. Look at the mess they've made." I pointed to the crumbs that were scattered across the carpet.

"When we have kids, you'll have to get used to a few crumbs."

"Back up a little. *When* we have kids?"

"Yeah. You can't have a tidy house when you've got children."

"I get that. I just missed the part where we'd talked about having them."

"I just assumed. You do want children, don't you?"

"I guess." I couldn't picture myself as a mum; I didn't feel mature enough. Time to change the subject—for now at least.

"I kicked your ass at the board games tonight, didn't I?"

"I still don't get how you won that first game of Snakes and Ladders." Jack scratched his chin. "I was sure that snake wasn't on that square."

"Poor loser, Jack. That's you."

Snigger.

Chapter 7

"Good morning, Jill," Megan shouted, as I stepped out of the house the next morning.

"Morning, Megan."

"Did I see Kathy and Peter come over to your house last night?"

"Yeah. We were babysitting for them while they went to see Murray Murray at the Washbridge Arena."

"Really? I'm jealous. I love that guy, but I couldn't get a ticket. Did they enjoy it?"

"Apparently."

"I thought about coming around to thank Peter for all the help he's given me. Without his assistance, I doubt I'd have so many clients already."

"You should have come over." Kathy's face would have been a picture.

"It was rather late, so I decided it would be better to thank him another time. Do you think he'd let me take him out for lunch or dinner some time?"

"I'm sure he would."

Stirring it? Who, me?

Before setting off in the car, I phoned the office.

"Jules, I thought I'd just let you know that Mrs V is feeling a lot better now."

"What was wrong with her?"

"I don't really know, but I'm positive she'll be back to her old self again the next time you see her."

"What time will you be in, Jill?"

"I'm not sure. I'm going to interview someone in connection with the case I'm working on. It's quite a long drive, so I'm not sure if I'll get in or not. I'll keep you posted. If there are any important messages, you can give me a call."

"Okay, Jill."

Before I could set off, my phone rang. It was Mad.

"Jill, I have news about the client that Lester despatched to the wrong destination."

"Is it good news?"

"Yes. I managed to track down the paperwork, and just as I'd hoped, the man was still in the holding area waiting to go on his journey. It was lucky for us that there's such a backlog at the moment. I grabbed the paperwork, and had a word with one of the officials, who has agreed to amend it. Lester's client will now be going via Ghost Town."

"Are you absolutely sure?"

"Yeah. One hundred percent. Lester is off the hook."

"Thanks, Mad. I owe you one."

"See you at the wedding, then."

"The wedding?" I'd tried to blank that out of my mind. "Oh, yeah. See you there."

***

When Andrew Clowne had visited my offices, he'd mentioned that two clowns had been murdered in the last year. From the details he'd given me, I'd managed to track down articles related to those deaths. I thought it might help the investigation if I could speak to those connected to the murder victims.

The first death was a clown who had gone by the name of Bongo. He had been part of a double act: Bingo and Bongo. His partner, Bingo, lived in Corndale—a two-hour drive from Washbridge. I'd managed to contact him by phone, and he'd agreed to speak to me about Bongo's death.

On arriving in Corndale, I found Manors Road using the GPS. The house was easy enough to spot; it was painted all the colours of the rainbow. On the front door, where one might normally have expected to find a knocker, there was a big red nose. I bet the neighbours loved this guy.

It took me a few seconds to work out that the big red nose was actually the doorbell. As soon as I pressed it, there was a loud peel of bells. It sounded as though there was an army of bell ringers inside. The man who opened the door was wearing large clown shoes, white baggy trousers and a string vest. The left side of his face was covered in something creamy white in colour.

"You must be Jill Gooder."

"That's me. I'm sorry if I've caught you in the middle of rehearsing."

He looked puzzled.

"The custard pie." I pointed to his face.

"That's shaving foam." He laughed. "Take a seat in the living room while I finish shaving, would you?"

The living room was unlike any I'd seen before. The walls were covered in photographs of clowns, which was terrifying enough. But to make matters worse, there was a glass showcase with the head and shoulders of a clown in it. The first time it started to laugh, I almost jumped out of my skin. Imagine living with that thing? The one thing missing from the room was a seat of any kind. Instead, there were several colourful barrel-shaped objects.

A few minutes later, Bingo returned, clean-shaven.

"Do take a seat," he said.

I couldn't work out where I was meant to sit until he walked up to one of the barrel-shaped objects, and lowered himself backwards onto it. Only then, did I realise that the 'barrels' were made of some kind of foam material which shaped to your body when you sat on them.

I followed his lead, and lowered myself onto the orange barrel. It was surprisingly comfortable.

"Thank you for seeing me today, Bingo."

"Bingo isn't my real name. That's just my stage name."

"Of course. What should I call you?"

"Coco."

I laughed.

He didn't. He just looked puzzled. "My name is Coco Smith, but I could hardly use Coco as my stage name, could I?"

"I guess not."

"I needed a more clown-like name. That's when I came up with Bingo."

Oh boy!

"I see. And your ex-partner? I assume Bongo was his stage name too?"

"No. His name was Arthur Bongo."

I couldn't decide whether this guy was having a laugh at my expense or not, but I decided to go with it for now.

"Well, Coco, I wonder if you could tell me what happened to your partner?"

"It was all rather tragic. Both of us had full time jobs. The clown act was just a hobby which earned us a little pocket money. For the most part, we relied on slapstick humour—you know: custard pies in the face, buckets of water over the head, that kind of thing. We both wanted to add something to the act that would grab the attention of the audience. We'd been looking around for some time when we found the ideal prop: a clown car."

"Wasn't that rather expensive if this was only a hobby?"

"It's not a real car; you can't actually drive it. It doesn't even have an engine. It's simply a wooden-framed prop in the shape of a car. The idea was that Bongo would sit in the front, I would sit in the rear, and we would do our routine as though we were driving along. There were many comedy features built into the car. For example, the wheels would drop off, and the steering wheel would come away in Bongo's hand. But the piece de resistance was the front seat, which was fitted with an ejector mechanism. It was designed to shoot the driver out of the car and onto the floor. But something went badly wrong."

He took a deep breath, and I could see he was trying to hold back the tears. I gave him a few moments, and then gently prompted him.

"I'm sorry to upset you, but it would be really helpful if you could tell me exactly what happened."

"Sorry. We were in Bongo's garage, testing the new prop before we used it in our live act. Everything seemed to be working fine. The wheels fell off, and the steering wheel came away in Bongo's hand. The only thing we had left to test was the ejector seat. Bongo put his foot on the brake pedal, which was the trigger. It shot him up into the air, and he hit his head on the roof of the garage. He was killed instantly."

"That's terrible. I'm very sorry for your loss. Can I ask where you got the clown car from?"

"We'd been looking for one for ages, and eventually

found it on Clown's List."

"What's that?"

"It's an online marketplace specifically for clowns."

"Have the police made any progress with the investigation?"

"The police aren't investigating the death."

"Do they already know who the murderer is?"

"Murderer? This wasn't murder; it was just a terrible accident."

"So the police aren't involved?"

"No."

I thanked Bingo for his time, but was now more confused than ever. Andrew Clowne had told me that the extortionist had stated that he had been responsible for two murders—the first of which was that of Bongo. And yet, the local police weren't treating this death as murder at all. Maybe things would look clearer after I'd had the opportunity to speak to the partner of the second 'murder' victim.

***

It was ages since I'd taken Barry for a walk, and the guilt was getting to me. After I'd driven back to Washbridge, I parked my car, and then magicked myself over to Candlefield.

"Great news!" Lester greeted me when I walked through the door. "I've just heard that I've been reinstated."

Aunt Lucy was standing directly behind him; she didn't appear to share his excitement.

"That *is* great news," I said.

"Did you have anything to do with it, Jill?" he asked.

"I had a word with Mad. She managed to track down the paperwork, and got it amended before the client had been transported."

"Thank you." Lester gave me a hug.

"Yes, thanks *very much*, Jill." Aunt Lucy said, with no sincerity whatsoever.

"I'd better get going." Lester started for the door. "I promised to meet Monica in twenty minutes."

"Bye then, Lester." I called after him, then turned around, to find Aunt Lucy giving me an icy glare. "What was I supposed to do? He seemed so unhappy."

"You're right—I know. I just hate that job of his. Shall we have a cup of tea?"

"Not right now, thanks. I thought I'd take Barry out for a walk. It's ages since I did that."

"Good idea. He's in the back garden. I let him out a few minutes ago, to do his business."

I went outside, but there was no sign of Barry anywhere. Then I noticed the back gate was open.

"Aunt Lucy! He's gone!"

She came rushing out of the back door, looked left and right, and then spotted the open gate.

"Oh no! I'm so stupid. I must have left it open when I put the bin out."

"Where do you think he might have gone?"

"I don't know. Maybe to the Park? It's his favourite place, and he definitely knows his way there."

"Okay." I headed for the gate. "I'll go there. You check the streets around here."

I ran all the way. By the time I reached the park gates, I was exhausted. If anything had happened to Barry, I'd never forgive myself.

To my relief, as soon as I walked through the gates, I spotted him in the distance.

Phew!

But then, I spotted another Barry, and then another, and another, and yet another. The park was full of black and white Labradoodles.

"Are you all right?" A woman wearing a black coat and a white headscarf walked over to me. "You look a little upset?"

"I've lost my dog. I thought that was him at first, but then I saw all the others. I don't understand what's going on here."

"Is your dog a black and white Labradoodle, by any chance?"

"Yes."

"I can see why you might be confused then. It just so happens that today is the bi-weekly meeting of BWLC."

"BWLC? What's that?"

"The Black and White Labradoodle Club. My name is Jessica Dewdrop; I'm president of the club. Have you tried calling your dog?"

"Barry! Barry!" I yelled at the top of my voice. "Come here, boy!"

Suddenly, two black and white Labradoodles came rushing towards me.

"Oh dear," Jessica Dewdrop said. "Is your dog's name Barry?"

"Yes."

"Barry is the single most popular name with our members. We have at least five Barrys in our club."

I was beginning to despair, but then I noticed a familiar

face in the distance. It was Dolly, Dorothy's mother. With her were two dogs: Barry and Babs.

I dashed over to them. As soon as Barry saw me, he began to pull on the lead. So much so, that Dolly had to let him go.

He came rushing over, jumped up, and almost flattened me.

"Jill! I didn't know you were coming today!" he said, excitedly.

"What were you thinking, Barry?" Who was I kidding? Thinking wasn't exactly Barry's strong suit. "You shouldn't have come here by yourself. We've been worried about you."

"I'm okay. I know my way to the park. I met Babs."

"So I see."

"There are lots of other dogs in here today that look just like me."

"I know. Apparently, it's a club for black and white Labradoodles."

"Can I join?"

"Would you like that?"

"Yes, please. Can I? Can I?"

"I suppose so. You stay here while I go and sign you up." I handed his lead back to Dolly.

"Excuse me!" I called to Jessica Dewdrop.

"Did you find your dog?"

"Yes, thanks. That's him over there."

"Jolly good."

"I'd like to sign up for your club, if I may?"

"Certainly. We're always on the lookout for new members." She took a sheet of paper out of her bag. "This is the application form. You'll need to complete this, and post it to the address on the bottom, along with your first monthly fee."

"Fee?"

"We have to levy a small fee to cover overheads: admin and the like."

"Of course." I took the form from her.

"We'll see you at the next meeting, then."

"I'll look forward to it."

As Jessica Dewdrop went back to join the other club members, I glanced at the application form. What? It cost how much?

"Did you sign me up?" Barry asked when I got back to him.

"It's an awful lot of money."

"Aww, please, Jill. Aren't I worth it?"

"Oh, go on then. I suppose so."

I'm too soft-hearted, that's my problem.

Chapter 8

Jack and I had had a quiet weekend at home. On Saturday, we'd worked on the garden. On Sunday, Jack had washed both cars while I caught up on my beauty sleep. Then we'd gone out to a local carvery for Sunday lunch.

"The garden's looking much better," I said, as we ate breakfast on Monday morning.

"No thanks to you."

"What do you mean? It was a joint effort."

"Sitting on the bench, barking orders, does not constitute a joint effort."

"I was supervising."

He rolled his eyes. "And how come I get to wash *both* cars?"

"You're so much better at it than I am."

"You can wash them next time."

"Sure. No problem." I'd already had a chat to the young boy from two doors down. He'd said he'd do them both for a fiver.

Jack left for work before me. When I stepped out of the front door, Mr Hosey had parked his silly little train right outside Jen's house, and he appeared to be treating her to one of his illuminating lectures. I know it was cruel of me, but I couldn't help but think that was karma. After all, she and Blake had escaped to the movies to avoid Hosey's dreadful open day—the same one that Jack and I had been forced to suffer.

"Jill! Jill." Jen came rushing across the road, leaving Mr Hosey looking rather put out. "Rescue me, please! He's been talking to me for the last fifteen minutes, and I don't seem to be able to get rid of him. I told him that I'd promised to give you something this morning." She held out her hand as though she was passing something to me, and then said in a whisper, "Pretend to take it."

I did as she asked. "It's okay." I gestured across the road. "He's leaving."

"Thanks, Jill, you're a lifesaver. That man is impossible. He just can't take a hint."

"I don't know what you're complaining about. Jack and I had to endure his open day."

"You're kidding." She laughed. "You're not telling me that you actually went over to his place, did you?"

"Unfortunately, yes. It was the longest night of my life, and it was all Jack's fault."

Jen double-checked to make sure that Mr Hosey had gone. "I suppose I'd better be making tracks. I'm already late for work because of that nutjob. How about you and I grab a coffee later today, Jill? Could you make it at lunch time?"

"Yeah. I'd like that. Where did you have in mind?"

"How about Coffee Triangle?"

"Fine by me."

"Okay, shall we say one o' clock?"

"Sure. I'll see you there."

"By the way, our new neighbour has moved in already."

"That was quick. Have you met them yet?"

"I think it's just a 'him'. I haven't seen anyone else."

***

As I drove into Washbridge, I noticed a small film crew outside Betty and Norman's shop. There was quite a crowd gathering to see what was happening, and being the nosy kind of person I am, I decided to take a look for myself.

After parking the car, I made my way on foot down the high street. Norman was standing in front of the shop window being interviewed by a man dressed in a suit with an unusual polka dot design. It was only when I got closer that I realised that the polka dots were actually pictures of bottle tops. Betty was inside the shop, standing by herself behind the counter. She didn't look particularly happy.

"Good morning, Betty."

"Morning, Jill." She sounded as fed up as she looked.

"It looks like you're getting some nice free publicity for the shop."

"Not the kind of publicity I would have liked." She sighed. "It's Toppers TV."

"As in bottle toppers?"

"Yeah. They're doing a feature on Norman and the shop. It's scheduled to go out tonight at prime time."

"Surely, that's a good thing? Why the long face?"

"We already have more than enough toppers coming into the shop. There's barely room for my customers to get through the door. After this article has aired on Toppers TV, we'll be overrun."

"But, you two are in it together now, aren't you?"

"I suppose so, but it's all so very disappointing. When I left HMRC, it was to pursue my dreams. When I opened She Sells, I couldn't have been happier. Now it just feels like I'm a bit player. All the attention is on Norman and his stupid bottle tops."

"He did put a lot of money into the shop." Even if he didn't know it at the time.

"I know, and I'm grateful for that. I'm just not sure that I can carry on with things as they are. If one more person asks me about the Blue Diamond bottle top, I'll hit them over the head with a crustacean."

As I was leaving the shop, the interview with Norman had just come to an end. The TV presenter, with microphone in hand, was looking around the crowd for someone else to speak to when he spotted me.

"This young lady appears to be one of the first customers of this exciting new shop." The man stuck the microphone under my nose. Standing behind him, was a skinny young man holding a camera, which was pointed directly at me. For a moment, I thought about telling him that I had no interest at all in bottle tops, but then I figured I might as well have some fun.

"So, young lady. What's your name?"

"Liliana Topps."

"Topps, eh? With a surname like that there's little wonder that you're a fan of the bottle top."

"I guess so." I giggled.

"What do you think of this new shop, Liliana?"

"I'm so excited about it. I live and breathe bottle tops. I even dream about them. Last night I dreamt that I'd found a Blue Diamond at the bottom of my garden. Can you imagine how excited I was?"

"That would have been quite something, wouldn't it? Have you bought anything today, Liliana?"

"No. I've just been browsing. But I have to say that

Norman does have one of the best stocks of bottle tops in the country. We're so lucky to have this new shop here in Washbridge. I do hope that everyone will support Norman and Betty in their new venture. Particularly Betty who I know is extremely excited at this addition to her original shop."

I glanced to my left, and caught sight of Betty who was scowling at me.

Whoops!

***

I had never seen so many scarves and socks in one place in my life. When I walked into the office, I could barely see the floor because it was covered with them. Standing in the middle of this sea of yarn was Mrs V.

"Good morning, Jill. Isn't it a beautiful day?"

"What's going on, Mrs V?"

"Well, dear, I've had so much sleep over the last few days that I can't remember the last time I felt so vitalised. I thought I'd take advantage of all this excess energy and do a stocktake."

"Of your socks and scarves?"

"Precisely. I've lost track of just how many I have, so I've decided to sort them by size and colour, and then make an inventory of them. I'm going to use that thing on the computer. What is it called, again? A data vase, I think."

"You mean database."

"That's the one."

"Isn't that a little ambitious?"

"Not at all. Jules was kind enough to give me a few tips,

and I think I get it."

"Might it be time to get rid of a few of these scarves and socks? There are an awful lot of them."

"But then I wouldn't have anything to give to your clients, would I? What would they think?"

"I hadn't considered that. Still, maybe you could keep a few at your house?"

"Oh no, dear. Much better to keep them all in one place."

I was fighting a losing battle. "Do you think you could make me a cup of tea?"

"Not at the moment, Jill. I have my hands full, as you can see."

"Yes. Of course. Sorry."

As soon as I walked into my office, I went straight to the cupboard, and took out a tin of salmon. Red not pink, obviously.

"There you go, Winky." I put the bowl onto the floor. "Cream?"

"Just a smidgen." He had a stupid smirk on his face. That was always a little disconcerting. I had a feeling that he was up to something, but I couldn't figure out what.

After he'd finished his salmon and cream, he jumped onto my desk. "I've been thinking."

That was never a good sign. "Yes?"

"You seem to have been getting more cases recently."

"That's true. Word must be spreading at last."

"I thought that maybe you could do with more help?"

"I've already got Mrs V and Jules. I don't think I need any more assistants."

"I was thinking more in terms of management help.

Someone to oversee the big picture."

"I don't know. Finding the right person would be very difficult."

"That's where I might be able to help you."

"Really?"

"Yes. I've been giving this some careful thought, and I'm prepared to become your partner."

"How do you mean?"

"You would continue to do all the investigative work, the old bag lady and Jules would do all the admin, and I would be responsible for strategic planning."

"That's a brilliant idea, Winky. I should have thought of it before."

"Good, that's decided then. I'll put together a partnership agreement for you to sign, and then we can start to split the profits. What do you say?"

"That sounds fantastic. If you get the paperwork sorted, I'll sign it."

***

I'd arranged to meet Jen at Coffee Triangle. It was maracas day so we didn't have to worry about the noise levels. While I was waiting for her, I spotted something on the noticeboard. The management had issued an apology for the ill-fated wind instrument experiment. They reassured customers that from now on they would be sticking to their original remit to include only percussion instruments. I was sure that would come as a great relief to everyone.

When Jen arrived, we queued together. I ordered a cappuccino; she went for an Americano. We both indulged in muffins: mine was the obligatory blueberry, Jen went for the chocolate chip. We found a quiet corner booth away from the maracas playing hordes.

"Do you come here often, Jill?" Jen took a bite of her chocolate chip muffin.

"At least twice a week, but I try to avoid gong and drum days."

"I thought I should let you know that Blake and I have been getting on much better recently."

"So, you're not still worried that he might be seeing someone else?"

"No. I'm now absolutely sure that he's been faithful to me."

"That's good."

"I did just want to clear one thing up though." Jen picked at her fingernail as though she was a little nervous. "The other night when the guys had gone bowling, and we were having a drink at your place, I hope I didn't say anything out of turn."

"You didn't."

"I know I had rather more wine than I should have. Sometimes, when I drink too much, I can shoot my mouth off."

"No. Nothing like that."

"So, I didn't say anything about Blake being—err—able to do magic, or anything like that, did I?"

"Not that I recall."

"Good. And, I didn't mention wizards?"

Jen was digging herself into a deeper and deeper hole with every word.

"Wizards?" I laughed. "Why would you mention wizards?"

"No reason. I just wouldn't want you to think I believed in wizards because obviously, there's no such thing. Or any other paranormal creatures for that matter."

"Of course not. That would just be silly."

It was obvious that Blake had told Jen to be careful what she said, but unfortunately it had had precisely the opposite effect. In trying to cover her tracks, Jen was making matters even worse.

"Have you spoken to your new neighbours yet?" It was time to get off the subject of wizards.

"I did try. I called to him but either he didn't hear, or he just ignored me. He's a bit of an oddball. But then again, I guess he can't be any worse than Mr Hosey."

Chapter 9

"Is that you, Jill?"

When Grandma telephoned me, it was usually bad news.

"Yes, Grandma, it's me." Who else was it going to be on my mobile?

"I hate using this stupid phone. I don't know why you don't open your telepathic channel, so I can contact you directly."

Ever since I'd read Magna Mondale's book, Grandma had been pestering me to open my telepathic channel, which would allow her to contact me telepathically at any time. Not likely! Just the thought of it was horrifying.

"Can you get down to Ever, right now?"

"I've got quite a lot of work on at the moment, Grandma."

"That isn't important. This is. Get down here right now."

She didn't give me an opportunity to argue because she'd already hung up. I could have ignored her request, but if I had, it would have come back to bite me on the bum.

There was a crowd of people standing outside Ever, looking at the dragon. Inside, there was only one customer, who was studying the racks of patterns. Kathy was behind the counter, but didn't notice me come in. She seemed to be miles away in a world of her own. There was a lot of banging and crashing coming from somewhere above our heads.

"What's all the noise?" I had to wave my hand in front

of Kathy's face to get her attention.

She shook her head as though she couldn't hear me.

"I said what's all the noise." I pointed to the ceiling.

Then I realised why she couldn't hear—she had earplugs in. "What did you say?" She removed them.

"I said what's all that noise?"

"It's been driving me crazy. It's your grandmother's latest brainwave. She's decided that what Ever A Wool Moment needs is a roof terrace and garden."

"Why?"

"The tea room is quite often full, and there's nowhere to expand on either side, so your grandmother came up with the brilliant idea of expanding onto the roof."

"Hasn't she seen the weather in Washbridge?"

"I tried to tell her, but you know what she's like. She doesn't listen to anyone. She said the weather wouldn't be a problem."

"I see the dragon is still attracting a lot of attention."

"I don't like that thing." Kathy shuddered. "It scares me."

"How do you mean?"

"It's weird. There doesn't seem to be any way to turn it off. I've looked everywhere, but I can't see any cables leading to the glass cage. I'd planned to switch it off when I went home at night, to save electricity, but it doesn't appear to be plugged in anywhere."

That more or less confirmed my fears that the dragon was actually a real one, which Grandma had brought from Candlefield.

"Maybe they have some kind of internal battery." I was clutching at straws to come up with an explanation that would satisfy Kathy. "It's remarkable what they can do with batteries these days."

"I guess that must be it. I hadn't thought of that. By the way, have you seen this?" Kathy pointed to a flyer on the noticeboard. "We have a celebrity coming to the shop."

The flyer announced that Kirsten Bracken, Miss Triple-loop herself, would be visiting Ever. She would be giving a talk on the triple-loop stitch, and would then be available for a Q and A, followed by autograph signing. Admission would be ten pounds.

"Grandma is charging an admission fee?"

"What else would you expect?" Kathy shrugged. "When she first told me about it, I assumed admission would be free, but your grandmother scoffed at that idea. She said that they'll be queueing down the street, and that ten pounds was a bargain."

"When you two have done gossiping on my time," Grandma shouted from the back office. "I'd like a word please, Jill!"

"Her master's voice. I'd better go. See you later, Kathy."

Kathy replaced the earplugs, and went back to work.

"Take a seat!" Grandma pointed to the chair opposite her desk.

I did as I was told. "Are you sure that dragon in the window is safe?"

"Of course it's safe. Perfectly safe. It can't get out of that cage; it's made of reinforced glass. Don't waste your time worrying about trivial things like my dragon. There's something much more serious that you should be concerned about."

"What's that?"

"Word is going around that a witchfinder has moved to Washbridge." She looked genuinely worried, and there wasn't much that worried Grandma.

"Witchfinder? I thought they only existed in bad b-movies?"

"As usual, young lady, you are misinformed. Witchfinders are very real indeed, and they pose a serious threat to every witch in Washbridge."

"What exactly do witchfinders do?"

She rolled her eyes and sighed. "Surely the name gives it away? Witch? Finder? What do you think they do? Herd sheep? They find witches, of course."

"I'd worked that much out, but what do they do once they've found a witch?"

"Destroy her. Witchfinders are extremely powerful, and can kill even the most powerful witches."

I didn't like the sound of that. Not one bit. "So how are we meant to stop them?"

"The only way to stop a witchfinder is with Brewflower."

"Isn't that what Alicia used to poison me just before the Levels Competition?"

"Exactly."

"But I thought it was banned?"

"It is, and normally I wouldn't advocate using it. But it's the only thing that will stop a witchfinder."

"You mean kill them?"

"No. They're too powerful for it to kill them, but it will weaken them to the point where they're no longer a threat."

"How will I recognise this witchfinder?"

"It isn't easy. The only way to be sure that someone is a witchfinder, is to look for a tattoo at the nape of the neck."

"What kind of tattoo? Does it say 'Witchfinder'?"

"Yes, it says 'Witchfinder' in big red letters." She sighed in obvious exasperation. "Of course, it doesn't. It's a small tattoo of a goblet."

"Why a goblet?"

"How would I know? I don't get invited to the annual witchfinder dinner and dance. You must be extra vigilant. Be suspicious of every new person who comes into your life. If the rumours are true, and there really is a witchfinder here in Washbridge, then you can bet he'll be seeking out the most powerful witches, and that means you and me. We'll be at the top of his list of targets, so you must be extra careful. Got it?"

"Got it."

As I walked back to the office, I found myself staring at everyone, wondering if they might be the witchfinder. And, I kept checking behind me, just in case I was being followed. If it had been Grandma's intention to scare me, she'd certainly succeeded.

Before going back to the office, I knew that there was something else I needed to do, but I couldn't for the life of me remember what it was. Then it came to me. I needed to buy more salmon for Winky. I popped into the minimarket which was a few doors down from my office, picked up a basket, and filled it with tins of red salmon.

The woman at the checkout gave me a curious look. "You're going through a lot of salmon, recently?"

"Sorry?"

"This is the second time you've been in this week and bought a basketful of it."

"I have? Oh, yes. I'm having a party at the weekend, and all the guests are big fans of salmon."

"They must be."

Once I was out of the shop, I thought about what the woman had said. I had been buying an awful lot of salmon, but had no idea why. I'd bought a lot of cream too. Why on earth had I bought so much? It was almost as though I'd felt compelled to do it.

And then something occurred to me.

Winky had been studying hypnosis. I had pooh-poohed the whole thing because I'd always thought hypnosis was bogus. But I'd obviously been wrong. He must have hypnotised me so that I'd buy him lots of salmon and cream. And that wasn't all. The conversation we'd had the previous day came back to me. He'd suggested he become a partner in the business, and I'd gone along with it, and agreed, in principle, to split the profits fifty-fifty.

That sneaky little so-and-so! How dare he use his mind control on me? I was seething, so instead of going back to the office, I went home. I needed time to plan my revenge on my darling little hypnotist.

***

As I pulled onto the driveway, I spotted Jen and Blake's new neighbour standing in front of his house. Jen had said that he seemed a rather strange man, and I could see what she meant. He was wearing what appeared to be some kind of cloak. The hood was pulled down over his head, so the only part of his face I could see was his beard. Although I couldn't see his eyes, he appeared to be looking in my direction.

Maybe I was just being paranoid? Maybe he was just taking some fresh air?

"Hi!" I waved.

He didn't reply. In fact, he didn't respond at all.

Now, he was beginning to give me the creeps, and I remembered what Grandma had said about any strangers who came into my life. Could our new neighbour be the witchfinder? I turned on my heels, and hurried into the house as quickly as I could. Once inside, I went straight to the front window, and peered outside. He had disappeared.

Just then, the lounge door opened, and I almost jumped out of my skin. This was it! The witchfinder had come to get me.

"Jill? Are you all right?"

"Jack. It's you."

"Who did you think it was?" He looked worried. "Are you okay?"

"Yeah. You just made me jump, that's all."

What was I meant to say? I could hardly tell him that I'd thought he was the witchfinder, come to get me, could I?

"Didn't you see me pull onto the drive?"

I'd been so busy looking across the road that I hadn't noticed Jack's car pull up.

"No, sorry. I was miles away. You're back early?"

"I've had enough today. That place is driving me insane."

He took a seat on the sofa, but I stayed by the window, just in case the witchfinder made a move.

"Bad day?" I asked.

"I'm fed up of being given trivial work to deal with. I know that I'm the new guy over there, but seriously, some of the cases they've handed me recently are beyond a joke.

Take today—the boss passed me a missing person case. A man has gone missing; his wife reported it a couple of days ago. I interviewed her today, and you'll never guess what she told me?"

"What?" I was only half listening because I was still worried about the witchfinder.

"Get this. According to this crazy woman, her husband is a wizard."

Now, Jack had my full attention.

"A wizard?" I laughed.

"Yeah. A wizard. She reckons that some creatures, which she called retrievers, came from the supernatural world to take him back because he made the mistake of telling his wife that he was a wizard."

"That all sounds a bit crazy to me."

"Tell me about it. I had to take her statement. It took me all my time not to laugh out loud. And then she wanted to know what I was going to do about it. I'll tell you what I'd like to do about it—file it in the waste paper bin. There's no wonder her husband disappeared; he was probably glad to get away from that lunatic. Wizards? Whatever next?"

Chapter 10

I hadn't slept well at all. I'd been listening in case I heard any noises inside the house. I was worried that the witchfinder might try to get in, and attack me during the night. So, when it was time to get up the next morning, I was completely shattered.

"Are you okay, Jill?" Jack said, when he came out of the shower.

"I didn't sleep very well."

"Nightmares again?"

"No. I just have a lot on my mind, at the moment."

"You and I both need a proper holiday."

"I'm too busy. I've got a full caseload at the moment."

"You work too hard. We could both do with another break. I'd certainly like to get away from that crazy woman and her wizard husband."

"I'll have to see what I can do. Maybe in a few weeks' time."

Jack left the house before me. After he'd gone, I ate my breakfast in the lounge so that I could watch the house across the road. I'd considered telling Grandma about our new neighbour, but I wasn't one-hundred percent certain he was the witchfinder yet.

Mrs Rollo called to me when I stepped out of the door.

"Jill, I'm sorry to bother you. I just wondered if you'd had any joy with the timeshare thing?"

"Sorry, Mrs Rollo. I haven't had the chance to do much yet. I do know that the contact details on both the business card and leaflet are false, though. I promise I'll get onto it in the next day or so, and I'll let you know what I find out."

"Thanks. I know you're busy. I do appreciate your help."

I took one last glance across the road, then I checked the back seat of the car—just in case. I really was getting paranoid now.

***

I'd just crossed the toll bridge when I heard a siren. In my rear-view mirror, I could see flashing lights. A police car was right behind me; the driver was gesturing for me to pull over.

I was doing nowhere near the speed limit. Maybe one of my brake lights was out.

"Jill, I'm sorry to pull you over like this."

"Blaze? You scared me to death."

"Sorry, but I needed to get hold of you, and I knew this was the route you took to work."

"Is everything okay?"

"No. Daze is going to kill me." He looked terrified.

"Why? What's happened?"

"It's my own stupidity. Just before she left, Daze arrested Slippery Sam."

"Slippery who?"

"Sam. He's a snake shifter who specialises in robbing banks. We'd been after him for months, and on the day before Daze left for her holiday, she caught him. We took him back to Candlefield, and put him into one of the holding cells. Daze asked me to process the paperwork so she wouldn't miss her plane. Anyway, I totally forgot to put on the anti-shifter shackles. After I'd prepared the paperwork, and went back to the cell, it was empty. He'd turned into a snake, and made his escape. I'm sure he must be back here in Washbridge somewhere, but I've no idea where. If he's still on the loose when Daze comes back, she'll murder me."

"Do you have any idea at all where he might be?"

"Not really. I was hoping that you might be able to help."

"I'd love to, but I'm really busy just now."

"Please, Jill. If I don't find him, I think there's a good chance that Daze will fire me."

"Okay. I can't promise anything, but I'll do what I can."

"Thanks, Jill. I really appreciate it."

After I'd parked my car, I dropped into the same minimarket that I'd been in the day before. The woman at the checkout saw me, and shouted, "More salmon?"

"Not this time. There's something else I'm after today."

I told her what I was looking for, and she pointed me in the right direction.

Jules was behind her desk, and sitting next to her was Gilbert. I barely recognised him. The last time I'd seen him, his face had been covered in acne. The transformation was amazing. His face was now blemish free.

"It's Gilbert, isn't it?" I said.

"That's me. I hope you don't mind me visiting Jules for a few minutes."

"Not at all."

"Gilbert has a new job," Jules said. "He's working for 'Magical Skin Care'. He's part of their promotion team, aren't you Gilbert?"

He nodded.

"Well, I have to say that the product seems to have worked wonders for you," I said.

"Thanks." He smiled. "It really is amazing. I've tried every skincare product on the market, and none of them worked, but within twenty-four hours of applying Magical Skin Care, my acne had disappeared completely."

That all sounded way too good to be true.

"Where exactly does Magical Skin Care come from?" I asked.

"It's from a company called The Candle Import Company. They're a new operation, but based on the success of this product, I think they'll get very big very quickly."

Candle Import Company? Magical Skin Care? I was beginning to smell a rat. This had all the hallmarks of a magic potion. The question was, who had brought it from Candlefield to Washbridge?

When I walked into my office, Winky was on the windowsill, staring across the way. I hadn't seen him do that for quite some time—not since Bella's owners had moved out, and she'd been forced to relocate.

"What are you looking at, Winky?"

"A new feline has moved into Bella's old apartment. And she's smoking hot."

"You shouldn't even be looking. I thought you and Bella were 'forever'?"

"You know what she's like. She's always going on at me to improve my image, and I refuse point-blank to take another deportment or elocution lesson. So, I fear she and

I may be history."

"Have you managed to make contact with this new cat, yet?"

"No. Bella must have left her flags behind because I've seen this new feline waving them around, but she obviously doesn't know semaphore. She just seems to be waving them randomly."

"That could make life difficult."

"That's why I got to thinking. Maybe you could take this over to her."

He passed me a book.

"A Cats' Guide to Semaphore?"

"Yes. If you could get that to her, then hopefully we'll soon be able to communicate."

I dropped the book onto my desk. "There's something else we need to sort out first. I've looked over the partnership agreement that you gave me, and I'm happy to go ahead with it."

His ears pricked up at that, and he jumped down from the windowsill, scurried across the floor, and leapt onto my desk.

"Very sensible." He had a smug look on his face. "We both need to sign it, then."

I took out a pen, scribbled my signature on the bottom, and then passed him the pen.

Just as I'd hoped, he signed without even giving it a second glance.

"Great," he said. "Now what's the first strategic issue you'd like me to work on?"

"Here, take this." I passed him the carrier bag.

"What's this?"

"Look inside."

"Cleaning materials?" He looked puzzled. "What are these for?"

"You'll need those to clean this office from top to bottom."

"Clean the office? Who do you think I am? I'm your partner—responsible for strategic planning, not the cleaner."

"I think you'll find you are." I held up the sheet of paper he'd just signed. "Read this."

He snatched it from my hand.

"What's this? This isn't the partnership agreement I drafted."

"No. That's an agreement which states that unless you clean this office once a week from top to bottom, you don't get any salmon."

He was stunned into silence for a few moments, but then found his voice. "You tricked me. You made me think I was signing the partnership agreement."

"I did, didn't I? That'll teach you to hypnotise me."

"I don't know what you mean."

"Don't give me that. Why else would I keep buying baskets full of salmon? You thought you had me under your control, didn't you?"

"It's your own fault. I only did it to prove to you that hypnosis works."

"And, I'm happy to admit you were right. Tell me, how does it feel to be right, Winky?"

Snigger.

***

I'd put it off as long as I could, but I owed it to myself to at least give I-Sweat a chance. The free passes, which they'd given to Mrs V, Jules and me, only lasted for one month. Both Jules and Mrs V were taking full advantage of their passes. Thankfully, Mrs V had now worked out how to operate the treadmills, which meant that she could get on and off when she wanted to, rather than being stranded on there for hours at a time. Jules usually went around there during her lunch hour, and she was looking much better for it. I'd recently treated myself to a new leotard. The old one had been looking a little the worse for wear, and was rather a tight fit—it had obviously shrunk.

The receptionist at I-Sweat wore a badge with the name 'Goldie' on it. She greeted me with a sunny smile.

"Good morning, madam. Welcome to I-Sweat."

"Morning. I have a free pass."

She glanced at it. "Oh yes. You're entitled to use all the facilities with this. If you'd like to get changed, I'll get one of our instructors to take you through your initial session."

When I came out of the changing room, Brent was waiting for me.

"Jill? I was beginning to think that we were never going to see you."

"I've been rather busy."

"Not to worry. You're here now. I'm going to assign you to Gavin. He's our newest instructor, and very good he is too. Just hold on there a moment, will you?"

The man who returned with Brent was dressed all in white: T-shirt, shorts, socks and trainers. He had it all: a great physique, good looking, and long black hair that most women would have killed for.

"Jill, this is Gavin." Brent made the introductions.

Gavin stepped forward and offered his hand. He had a very firm grip.

"Nice to meet you, Jill." He had the sexiest voice ever. He could have made a fortune doing voice-overs.

"Nice to meet you too," I whimpered.

"I'll leave you to it then," Brent said.

"How long is it since you last did any exercise?" Gavin asked.

"It must be several weeks." Years more like.

"Not to worry. We'll soon have you back to peak fitness. First things first, though. I need to take you through a quick questionnaire to assess your current level of fitness, and to get an idea of your diet, etc. Is that okay?"

"Sure. Whatever you say, Gavin."

What? Who are you calling a sycophant? I was only trying to be helpful to the young man.

An hour later, I hobbled out of I-Sweat, along the corridor, and back to my office.

"Jill?" Jules came around the desk, and took my hand. "Are you okay?"

"Just about." I took a deep breath. "I've just had my first free session at I-Sweat. I didn't realise how hard it would be. Still, I did have a really good looking instructor to help me. His name is Gavin. Have you met him?"

"No, but then Brent did say that he had a new instructor starting this week, so perhaps that's him."

"Gavin said he'd be overseeing my training during the free trial period, so I guess I'll be seeing him again. If I ever recover."

Chapter 11

I had to try to find out who had conned Mrs Rollo out of her savings. Conmen like that were the scum of the earth. First port of call was my trusty friend, Google. I searched using the search terms: Washbridge, timeshare and scam, but that returned too many results, so I limited the search to the last three months. That gave me a much more manageable number of results to check. One thing I noticed immediately was that two of them were from the same website. I clicked on the first one, and it took me to a forum called Merry Widows of Washbridge.

It was a surprisingly active forum, with different sections for all manner of interests including: cooking, holidays and grandchildren. The two messages that had been returned by Google were both in the 'holidays' section. Both posts detailed similar scenarios to that described by Mrs Rollo. In both instances, they had been approached by someone at the door, who had persuaded them to hand over money for a timeshare at a price that was totally unrealistic. There were several replies within those threads, mostly from people commiserating with the two women who'd lost their money. A few heartless individuals had lambasted the women for being silly in handing over their money. I was sure both women already felt bad enough without such unhelpful, unfeeling responses. It became obvious that neither woman had managed to track down the perpetrator of this dastardly crime. Nor had they managed to retrieve their cash.

In order to send a message to the two women, I first had to register for the forum, which asked for various pieces of information including: name, address, and date of birth.

The instructions made a point of saying that all information provided would be held securely, and not made available to other users of the website. The only information which was mandatory was a valid email address, so I left the rest blank. I chose the screen name 'Custard Cream Boat'. Once my registration was complete, it was a simple process to send a private message to the two women, asking them to contact me. All I could do now was wait to see if I got any replies.

***

Winky had spent the last hour cleaning the office from top to bottom. And to be fair, he'd done an excellent job. He'd proven to be something of a whiz with a feather duster, and the sight of him riding on the vacuum cleaner had been something to behold.

"There's still a little dust on the windowsill." I pointed.

"No there isn't." He ran his paw across the surface. "This office is spotless."

"I'm only joking." I grinned. "You've done a very good job. You can have salmon on a couple of days next week."

"I should think so too." He walked over to the sofa, picked up his book on hypnosis, and dropped it into the waste paper bin. "Good riddance."

"I hope that will teach you not to try to get one over on me. You should know you can't outsmart me."

"I may have lost the battle." He jumped onto the sofa, clearly exhausted. "But I'll win the war."

Call me a big softy, but I felt a little guilty at having made him work so hard, so I decided to offer an olive branch.

"Winky!"

"What?" He opened his eyes. "I was almost asleep."

"Just to show there's no ill feeling, I'll take your semaphore book across the road to your new feline friend."

That made him sit up. "Thanks, Jill. You're not so bad after all."

I made my way over to the building where Bella had once lived. Only when I was standing outside the door of Bonnie and Clive's former apartment, did it occur to me that I hadn't thought this through properly. How exactly was I meant to deliver the book to Winky's new feline friend? I could hardly knock on the door, and tell the new residents that I had a book for their cat. I'd made a similar mistake once before when I'd tried to deliver flowers to Bella.

Fortunately, I spotted a cat flap in the front door of their apartment. They must have had it fitted recently because it hadn't been there when last I'd called. Result! I took the book out of my bag, and posted it through the flap.

"What do you think you're doing?" The stern voice came from behind me.

I got to my feet to find a security man standing there. He was looking at me more than a little suspiciously. "Were you trying to get through that flap?"

"Of course not. How could I fit through there?"

"What *were* you doing, then?"

"I've just posted a book through the cat flap."

"And why, pray tell, would you do that?"

"I borrowed it from the people who live here, and I was just returning it."

"Why didn't you just knock on the door, and give it to them?"

That was a very good question. Before I had the chance to come up with an answer, the security man had knocked on the door.

"There's no need to disturb them," I said.

"You stay right there. Let's see what they have to say about this."

A few moments later, the door opened, and a middle-aged man smoking a pipe, appeared in the doorway. "Yes? Can I help you?"

The security man stepped forward. "This young *lady* says that she's just posted a book through your cat flap. Can you confirm whether or not that's true?"

"The man with the pipe bent down, and retrieved the book. "It appears she's telling the truth." He studied it. "A Cats' Guide to Semaphore?"

"Is that your book?" The security guard asked the man.

"No. I've never seen it before."

Both men looked to me for an explanation.

"It belonged to the people who lived here before you. They lent it to me, but I don't have their new address."

"I see," the man with the pipe said. "In that case, I'll hold onto it. The next time we have mail to forward to them, I'll send it along."

"Thank you very much," I said. "That's very kind of you."

"Not at all." The man with the pipe closed the door.

"The next time you have anything to deliver to an apartment in this building, I'd be grateful if you would contact reception first," the security guard said.

"Yes, of course. I'll make sure I do that."

And with that, I made my way out of the building. Hopefully, Winky's new friend would get a chance to look at the book before it was forwarded to Bonnie and Clive, who would no doubt be more than a little surprised to receive it.

***

It was time to pay a visit to the widow of the second clown supposedly murdered by the extortionist. The woman's name was Gemma Tyson. I'd managed to contact her by phone, and she'd been quite happy to talk to me, although she had seemed surprised that I was in any way interested in her husband's death.

The Tyson house didn't have any of the clown paraphernalia, which I'd found at the house belonging to Coco, a.k.a. Bingo. It was a modest semi-detached house in a quiet neighbourhood. Gemma Tyson was a woman in her late forties or early fifties. She welcomed me with a friendly smile, and offered me a cup of tea. To my delight, she handed me an unopened packet of custard creams.

"I'm afraid these are the only biscuits I can offer you. I had planned to go to the supermarket earlier, but I had a problem with the dishwasher—that set me back a little."

"Not to worry. Custard creams are my favourite biscuit."

"Really? I'm not too fond of them myself, but my friend, Beryl Bobbins, is very partial to them. I usually keep a pack in just for her. Do help yourself to as many as you like."

That was a very dangerous thing to say to me. I took three, but then handed back the packet. I just didn't trust myself.

"Thank you for seeing me."

"No problem. I'm still not sure why you're interested in Robert's death."

"Was your husband a full-time clown?"

"Oh no." She laughed. "Robert was actually an undertaker."

I hadn't seen that one coming. "Really?"

"Yes, a lot of people were surprised when they found out about his double life. His day job wasn't exactly a barrel of laughs, as you can imagine. I think that's why Robert chose to be a clown in his spare time. He really loved it. He would have liked to have done it full-time, but there simply wasn't enough money in it."

"Where did he actually do his clown act?"

"Mainly at birthday parties. He didn't make much money at it—just enough to cover his expenses plus a little extra. He mainly did it for the pleasure he got out of it. He called himself Mr Laughs." She smiled at the memory.

"I'm sorry to drag this up, and I have no desire to upset you, but I wonder if you could tell me exactly how your husband died?"

"Robert liked to treat himself to new props every now and then. Something that he could use in his act. Nothing too expensive, you understand. Just small bits and pieces that he could incorporate into the act. He'd bought a new custard pie gun; it had a huge barrel which fired custard pies." She took a deep breath and was silent for a long moment. "I'm sorry, but the memory is still quite painful."

"I understand. Take your time."

"When the custard pie gun arrived, he asked if I'd help him to test it. We went around the back of the house where no one would see us. I didn't want to do it in the house because of the mess. Robert asked me to fire the custard pie at him, which I did. It went with such force that when it hit him in the face, he fell backwards and banged his head on the concrete step. I called the ambulance, but by the time they arrived, he was dead. The post-mortem said that he'd ruptured a blood vessel in his brain when his head hit the step."

"Did the police interview you about the incident?"

"Of course. After all, I'd been the one who fired the custard pie gun, which was what caused him to fall backwards. But they realised it was just a terrible accident, and they didn't take it any further. That doesn't stop me from feeling guilty every day. If only he'd stood a few feet further back, I'm sure the impact wouldn't have knocked him over."

"At any point did the police treat the death as anything other than an accident?"

"No. They were quite understanding, actually."

"Just one last question please, if I may? Where did your husband buy the custard pie gun from?"

"He got it off Clown's List. He bought most of his props from there."

***

I'd no sooner got back home than Blake pulled onto his driveway. Jack wasn't home yet, and neither was Jen, so this was my opportunity to catch Blake, and warn him about his new neighbour.

"Blake! Can we go inside for a minute?"

"Sure. Come on in."

"Shut the door, Blake. You don't know who might be listening."

"And I thought I was paranoid." He grinned. "Whatever's the matter?"

"It's your new neighbour."

"You mean weird guy? Have you seen that cloak he wears?"

"Yeah. Look, I can't be sure, but I have a horrible feeling that he might be a witchfinder."

"What makes you think that?"

"According to my grandmother, there's word on the street that a witchfinder has moved into Washbridge. If it's true, she thinks he'll be targeting the most powerful witches in the area, which unfortunately would be Grandma and me. The other day he was standing on his drive, staring at me. I shouted 'hello', but he didn't reply. It's got me freaked out."

"That is a bit worrying."

"No kidding. I'm terrified. I thought I'd better warn you. I'm not sure whether witchfinders come after wizards as well as witches."

"I don't know either, but I'm nowhere near as powerful as you are, so it probably isn't me he's after."

"We'll both need to keep our wits about us. If either of us spots anything suspicious we must let the other know as quickly as possible."

"Agreed."

Chapter 12

I'd heard back from one of the other timeshare scam victims. Mrs Padd had contacted me via the Merry Widows forum, and after a brief exchange of messages, I'd arranged to go to her house. She lived very close to Kathy—in fact only a couple of streets away.

"Mrs Padd?"

"You must be Jill. Do come in, and please call me Lily."

Lily Padd? Seriously?

"Come through to the living room, and take a seat."

In both the hallway, and the living room there were birthday cards on every surface. There were literally hundreds of them.

"I take it it's your birthday?" I gestured to the cards.

"No. My birthday isn't for another two months."

"Oh?"

"I just hate to take cards down, don't you?"

"I guess so, but then I don't get nearly as many as you do. A dozen if I'm lucky."

"These aren't all from my last birthday." She laughed. "Some of these have been up for almost ten years. I just can't bring myself to put them in a drawer."

"I see."

Oh boy!

"I must admit that it's getting a little difficult now because I'm running out of surfaces to put them on. My bedroom is full of them, and so is the dining room. There's only really the kitchen that's birthday card free. I have to decide whether to start putting cards in there too, or if perhaps it's time to put some away. What do you think, dear?"

That she was as nutty as a fruit cake.

"It's a difficult decision, Lily, I can see that. Anyway, as I mentioned in my messages, my neighbour, Mrs Rollo has also fallen victim to the same timeshare scam. I promised her that I'd investigate to see if I can track down the person responsible, which is why I wanted to speak to you today."

"I'll certainly do my best to help you, dear. This has come as a terrible shock. He's taken a good part of my savings, which I won't now be able to pass on to my children."

"How many children do you have, Lily?"

"Two—a boy and a girl. They're both grown up now with children of their own. That's why I was tempted by the timeshare offer. I thought it would be ideal for us all to go away as a family: me, my children, and my grandchildren. But now I realise that I've just been a silly old fool."

"You mustn't blame yourself. People like this man are very cunning. Can you tell me exactly what happened?"

"The man just turned up at my door one day. Normally, I'm very wary of anyone cold calling, but he was so utterly charming, and seemed genuine. I fell for it hook, line and sinker. He talked about holidays first, and asked about my children and my grandchildren. When he first showed me the brochure, I told him I wasn't interested, but before I knew it, he'd somehow persuaded me that it was a bargain I couldn't pass up."

"Did you give him a cheque?"

"No. I gave him cash. I don't know what I was thinking. It was so stupid."

"Was that the last you heard from him?"

"Yes. He promised to come back the next day with all the paperwork, but I never saw or heard from him again. I went straight to the police, and they said they'd investigate, but I haven't heard back from them since. I suppose they have more important matters to deal with. And then I received your message."

I asked Lily to describe the man. Her description pretty much matched the one that Mrs Rollo had given me, including the meaty smell.

After I left Lily's, I called at several houses on the same street including the two next-door neighbours. I asked whether they'd been approached by anyone selling timeshares, but no one had. I found that very telling. It seemed that whoever was perpetrating this scam had targeted his victims very precisely, as though he knew they'd be easy prey.

***

When I got back into Washbridge, the car park I normally used was full. Great! The next nearest was some distance from my office, and twice as expensive. To top it off, the only ticket machine that was working was at the other side of the car park from where I'd parked.

As I began the trek to the office, I passed by the Magenta Hotel. It was one of the most luxurious, and certainly one of the most expensive hotels in Washbridge. As I drew level with the main entrance, a stretch limo with tinted windows pulled up at the curb.

The man who emerged from the back seat of the car had tight curly hair, a tan which he hadn't got in this country, and was wearing mirrored sunglasses. He was dressed in an all-white suit complete with white shoes. He'd no sooner stepped out of the car than a cyclist appeared from nowhere. He came whizzing past me on the pavement, and ran into the white-suited man, sending him crashing to the floor. It soon became apparent that this had not been an accident. The cyclist had deliberately targeted the man, and was now rifling through the stricken man's jacket. The cyclist took the man's wallet, and then slipped the man's watch from his wrist.

It all happened so quickly that no one had time to react. The cyclist was already back on his bike, and making his getaway. The white-suited man, who still looked a little shaken, was being helped back to his feet by a passer-by.

I couldn't simply stand by and allow this to happen, so I cast the 'faster' spell, and gave chase. I caught the cyclist before he reached the end of the street, grabbed him by the collar, and pulled him backwards off the bike onto the ground. The bike went careering down the road, and crashed into a lamp post. After casting the 'power' spell, I knelt on the cyclist who was still winded from his fall.

"Let me go!" He gasped.

"You're not going anywhere."

The white-suited man was now back on his feet, brushing himself down. He still looked a little disorientated. Moments later, a police car came screeching around the corner, and came to a halt opposite where I was still pinning the man to the ground. While I'd been waiting for the police to arrive, I'd managed to retrieve the wallet and watch, and had slipped them into my pocket.

"Okay, madam," one of the officers said. "We know this scumbag. We'll take it from here. If you could give my colleague your name and address, we'll be in touch later to take a statement."

I released the man who was then handcuffed by the officer. Once the thief was in the back of the car, the second police officer took my details. Meanwhile, the white-suited man had walked down the street to join us.

"Mr Murray, it's a pleasure to meet you," the officer said. "I saw you in concert last night. The show was fantastic."

Then it clicked. The white-suited man had to be Murray Murray. The pop sensation that Kathy had been raving about.

Murray Murray gave the officer his contact details, and then the police car took the thief away.

"These are yours, I believe." I handed the watch and wallet back to Murray Murray.

"Thank you. I didn't think I'd see those again. It wouldn't have mattered so much about the wallet, but this watch was a present from my late father. I thought I'd lost it for sure, but then I saw you giving chase. How did you manage to catch him?"

"I do a lot of running."

"That was very dangerous. He could have hurt you."

"Not his kind. They're brave enough when it comes to stealing from someone, but they aren't so brave when it comes to a fight."

"Is there anything I can do to thank you?"

"Well, now you come to mention it, there is something."

***

I'd done my best to get out of it, but the twins had

insisted that I go to Cuppy C to witness the launch of Baking Reimagined. They'd certainly done a good job on the publicity front because the shop was almost as full as it had been for the Sweaty Boys' show. The crowd today was a mix of men and women, and thankfully no one was shouting for anyone to take their clothes off.

"Jill." Amber beamed. "Just look how many people are here."

"I know. It looks like Baking Reimagined has captured their imagination."

"See, Jill," Pearl said. "We do get it right sometimes."

"I wish you well, girls. So, when do I get to see the cakes?"

Amber checked her watch. "Right now. I'm so excited."

The twins went into the back of the shop, and returned with several trays, which they placed on the counter.

"There you go!" Pearl said, proudly.

I glanced at the empty trays. "When will you be bringing the cakes out?"

"They're there." Amber pointed to the trays. "Look. Don't they look delicious?"

"I especially like the look of the cupcakes," Pearl said.

Either I was losing my mind or the twins had lost theirs.

"But there's nothing—"

"Shush!" Pearl grabbed me by the arm and led me behind the counter.

"I don't get it," I said.

"Neither did we at first until the man from Emperor Baking Enterprises explained. Only those with a discerning palate are able to see the cakes."

Huh?

"Are you telling me that you and Amber *can* see them?"

I glanced again at the empty trays.

"Of course we can. And very delicious they look too. Now, you stay here while we hand them out."

"Ladies and gentlemen!" Amber called the crowd to order. "Thank you for coming today for the launch of Baking Reimagined. As you will have already read in the leaflets we handed to you when you arrived, this truly is the next generation of cakes. They are of course visible only to those with the most discerning of palates, but we're confident that all of our customers meet that criteria. Enjoy!"

I watched in total disbelief as the twins took the empty trays from table to table. It seemed I was the only one who didn't have a discerning palate because at each table the customers appeared to pick out a 'cake' from the tray. Everyone seemed delighted with the new Baking Reimagined range.

"There's nothing there!" A young boy's voice cut through the shop. A witch sitting at a window table had brought her young son with her. He was pointing to the empty plate his mother had placed in front of him. "I want a real bun!"

"It's right there, Jimmy." His mother looked a little embarrassed.

"No, it's not." The boy waved his hand over the plate to illustrate the point.

"The boy's right!" A wizard who was seated a couple of tables away shouted. "This is a con."

Amber and Pearl looked mortified.

"Please, everyone." Amber stepped forward. "You have to really focus to be able to see the—"

And then it started.

"I want my money back." A witch stood up.

"Me too." A wizard shouted.

Soon, everyone was demanding a refund, and the twins had no choice but to comply. Fifteen minutes later, the shop was empty except for the three of us.

Amber and Pearl looked totally dejected.

"Come on, girls," I tried to encourage them. "It isn't your fault that the people of Candlefield don't have discerning palates."

"We've been conned again, haven't we?" Amber said.

"How could we be so stupid?" Pearl had her head in her hands.

"It'll be okay." I tried to reassure them. "You did the right thing. You gave everyone a refund. But you really must stop trying these crazy new initiatives. Just concentrate on selling good quality cakes at reasonable prices. That's all anyone wants from you."

"You're right, Jill," Amber said.

"You're always right, Jill." Pearl sighed. "We really should listen to you in future."

You think?

Chapter 13

Fortunately, I hadn't seen anything of the witchfinder overnight. Sooner or later, I would have to tackle that problem head-on, but now wasn't the right time.

Jack was a lot happier because he'd been taken off the 'mad woman with a wizard for a husband' case, and given something a little more meaty to get his teeth into. That was why he'd gone into work early, while I was still in the shower. Before I set off for work I had a phone call to make.

"Jill?" Kathy sounded half asleep. "What's wrong? Why are you calling at this unearthly hour?"

"Can we meet tonight after work for a drink?"

"Since when do you and I meet for a drink during the week? Or ever for that matter?"

"I have a little surprise for you."

"I've seen your surprises before." She sounded sceptical. "Can't you tell me what it is?"

"No, but I can promise that you'll really like it. Can you meet me in Bar Piranha at six o'clock?"

"Okay. I'll get Pete to pick up the kids from school. He can make dinner for a change. Can't you give me just a little clue what the surprise is?"

"No, but I can guarantee that you'll thank me for it."

***

I needed to talk to the owner of Clowns' List. Both clown deaths had been as a result of equipment bought from that online marketplace. It turned out that the website was in fact run by a man named Todd Prince, from his bedroom. Unfortunately, he lived at the other end of the country. After I'd contacted him via email, and explained my interest, he'd invited me to visit his house, but that would have taken a lot of time and expense for what was probably going to be a very short discussion. I did have the option to use magic to transport myself there, but I tried only to do that in an emergency.

It was Todd who came up with the bright idea that we could speak on Skype. I'd readily agreed, and we'd arranged to make contact that morning at nine-thirty.

But there was a problem. My antiquated desktop computer had decided it no longer wanted to run Skype. When I tried, it made a strange noise which translated to 'not today, sorry'. I couldn't even use the one in the outer office because it was waiting to be repaired. I think Jules must have fried it with her YouTube exploits.

It was nine fifteen. I had only fifteen minutes to come up with something. And then I remembered that Winky had a tablet. I'd seen him use it to communicate with Bella on Skype.

"Winky!"

He appeared from underneath the sofa, still half asleep.

"Do you still have your tablet? The one you used to talk to Bella on Skype?"

"Yep. Still got it."

"Do you think I could borrow it? I need to speak to someone in connection with the case I'm working on."

"You want to borrow my tablet?" He suddenly seemed more awake.

"Yes, please."

"What's it worth?"

"Salmon?"

"Nah. That doesn't really work for me."

"I've got to be online in fifteen minutes."

"In that case, you must be pretty desperate?"

What had I been thinking? Why had I let him know how urgent it was?

"What do I have to do for you to let me use it?"

"How about you rip up the agreement that I signed? The one where I have to clean the office?"

"No chance."

"Okay then." He disappeared back under the sofa.

He had me just where he wanted me, and he knew it.

"Okay, Winky. I agree."

He reappeared. "Go on, then. Rip it up."

I pulled open the drawer, took out the agreement which he'd signed, and tore it into shreds. "There. Are you satisfied now?"

"Sure." He reached underneath the sofa, grabbed the tablet, and jumped onto my desk.

"Nice doing business with you."

When I'd discovered that Todd Prince ran Clown's List from his bedroom, I hadn't realised that he did it while wearing his pyjamas. His interest in clowns was self-evident because his pyjamas were covered in them. So was the wallpaper behind him.

"Hello." He shouted at the screen.

"Hi. Thank you for agreeing to talk to me."

And then he began to pick his nose. Did he not realise how Skype worked? That I could see everything he was doing? I'll spare you the gory details.

"As I mentioned in my email, Todd, I'd like to ask you about the equipment that is sold on Clowns' List. Are you concerned that it could be dangerous?"

He stopped picking his nose for a moment — thank goodness. "Not at all. I suspect you're referring to the deaths of Bongo and Mr Laughs?"

"That's right."

"There really is nothing untoward. In both of those cases, the equipment sold was perfectly safe."

"How can you be sure of that?"

"It had been certified by the Clown Testing Labs."

"The what?"

"The Clown Testing Labs was set up by NOCA some years ago. Props are put through rigorous tests. Only those that pass are certified as safe. Those which fail, are confiscated."

"And you can check that a prop has been certified before accepting an ad?"

"Yes. It's easy to check online."

"So how come people died using these props?"

"Unfortunately, it appears that the buyers did not pay sufficient attention to the instructions that came with their purchases. In the case of Bongo, the clown car should only ever have been used in areas with plenty of headroom, such as outside or in a big top. It was never designed to be used inside somewhere like a garage. The ejector seat worked as designed, and if it had been in a big top it would have been perfectly safe. But because he was in a garage with a low ceiling, it proved to be fatal. As for Mr Laughs, the instructions stated quite clearly that under no circumstances should the gun be fired unless there was at least twelve feet between the barrel of the gun and the target. From what I understand, Mr Laughs' wife fired the gun from only three feet away. Even then, the force of the custard pie wouldn't have been enough to do serious damage, but unfortunately, he fell and hit his head on a step. Both were tragic accidents, but that's all they were. If the local press hadn't got hold of the stories, I doubt anyone would ever have heard about them."

He went back to picking his nose.

"Have the police been in touch with you at any stage?"

"Yes. In both instances, the police asked me to give them the seller's details, which I was happy to do. But I've since been in touch with both sellers, and they confirmed the police cleared them of all responsibility. This really is a non-story. How did you come across it, anyway?"

"I'm not able to discuss details of the case I'm working on, but I can tell you that there is a suggestion that these two deaths may have been murder."

He laughed. "That's just nonsense. They were accidents, plain and simple. Just ask the police."

I was glad to end the call. I'd seen enough of Todd Prince picking his nose to last me a lifetime. Was he some kind of nose-picking exhibitionist?

***

I arrived at Bar Piranha before Kathy. I still couldn't get my head around the changes they'd made to that place. When it first opened, it had been called Bar Fish, and had been a delightful place to visit. The tropical fish had brought the place to life, but now only piranhas occupied the tanks. The horrible creatures seemed to be staring out at me as though they were contemplating their next meal.

I ordered an orange juice. Kathy didn't arrive until just before six fifteen.

"I'm sorry Jill. Your grandmother collared me just as I was on my way out of the door. I told her that I'd arranged to meet you at six, but she said that you could wait."

"Typical Grandma. Was it anything important?"

"No. She wanted to know where the key was to get into the front window of the shop. I think she was going to clean out the dragon display."

"Clean it out?"

"It's really weird. The bottom of the cage keeps filling with what looks like white cotton wool balls. I'd offered to clean it out earlier in the day, but she said I wasn't to touch it because I might break something. It's nice to know she has such faith in me. Anyway, don't let's talk about your grandmother. I have enough of her during the day. I'm dying to know what the surprise is."

"Your surprise will be here in—" I checked my watch. "About ten minutes."

"Come on, Jill. Tell me what it is."

"No. Go and get a drink. You'll see soon enough."

Kathy went to the bar, and ordered herself a gin and tonic.

"Well?" Her patience was almost exhausted.

I took a slow sip of orange juice. "Not long now."

"You must be Kathy," a man's voice said.

Kathy spun around to find Murray Murray standing behind her. Her face was a picture. "Murray?" She finally managed. "Murray?"

"Would you two ladies mind if I joined you?" He was wearing a black suit today.

"Please do." Kathy patted the seat next to her.

"See, I told you you'd like your surprise," I said.

"But—err—I—how?" Kathy could barely string two words together. She was too busy ogling Murray Murray.

"Your sister, Jill, came to my rescue yesterday."

"She did?" Kathy glanced at me, but then quickly looked back at Murray Murray.

"Someone deliberately ran into me with a bike, and then stole my wallet and watch, but Jill gave chase, and retrieved them."

"It was nothing," I said, with false modesty.

"Anyway," Murray Murray continued. "I asked Jill if there was anything I could do by way of thanks, and she said she thought you'd like it if I joined you for a drink."

"I'm so glad you did!" Kathy gushed. "Me and my husband came to see you the other evening at Washbridge Arena. You were fantastic."

"Thank you. It's very kind of you to say so. I've taken the liberty of bringing my latest album for you." He took a CD out of his pocket. "Would you like me to sign it?"

"Yes, please. Could you write: 'To Kathy with love, Murray Murray'?"

"I'd be delighted."

I'd expected Murray Murray to rush away as soon as he'd finished his drink, but he stayed and chatted for almost an hour. We were interrupted every now and then when someone recognised him, and came over to have a selfie taken with him, or to ask for an autograph. Murray Murray handled it all with style.

"I really do love this area of the country," Murray Murray said. "In fact, if I could find the right house, I'd probably buy a home here. It would be a good place to get away from London. Unfortunately, I've looked around a few times, but nothing really caught my eye."

"Funny you should say that," I said. "I might know just the place for you."

***

Murray Murray had eventually made his excuses and left because he had a show later that evening. Kathy was still beside herself with excitement. I was now her favourite person in all the world for having introduced her to her idol. I wondered how long that would last. Not long, if I knew Kathy.

She and I had no sooner said our goodbyes than my phone rang. It was Grandma. This was becoming something of a habit, and one I could have done without.

"Hello, Grandma."

"Jill. You need to get down to Ever straight away. It's an emergency."

"What's wrong this time?"

The line was already dead, so I hurried over there as fast as I could. The first thing I noticed was that the glass cage in the front window was empty.

"Where's the dragon, Grandma?"

"It got away." She looked distraught; the wart on the end of her nose was throbbing red like some kind of beacon.

"What do you mean, 'got away'?"

"Just what I said."

"How?"

"I let it out so I could clean the cage, and somehow it got out of the front door."

"Hadn't you locked it?"

"I thought I had."

"Where is it now?"

"If I knew that, I wouldn't be asking for your help, would I?"

"Is it dangerous?"

"Of course it's dangerous. It's a dragon."

"It's only a baby though, isn't it?"

"It has very sharp teeth and claws, and it can breathe fire. How much more dangerous do you want?"

"Did you see which way it went?"

"It ran across the road towards that stupid sea shell shop."

"Sea shells and bottle tops, actually."

"Really? Do you think now is the time to quibble about exactly what rubbish that shop sells?"

"Sorry. You were saying?"

"I lost sight of it once it was on the other side of the road. You should be able to track it down because the cotton dragon leaves a trail wherever it goes." She pointed to the floor where there was a line of what looked like small, white cotton wool balls.

"Okay, you stay here in case it comes back. I'll follow this trail and try to track it down."

Chapter 14

Great! This was precisely what I wanted to be doing—chasing after a baby dragon. Fortunately, the trail of cotton wool balls was relatively easy to follow, but I'd need to act quickly because it would soon blow away, and if that happened, I'd never find the stupid creature. The white trail led down an alleyway, which ran between Betty and Norman's shop, and the hat shop next door.

That brought me out onto West Street. From there, the white trail led across the road to West Park. Before I could set off in pursuit, I heard a familiar voice.

"Jill? Are you all right?" It was Jules who was arm in arm with Gilbert—he of the perfect complexion.

"Oh? Hi, Jules. Yes, I'm okay." I glanced across the road. If I didn't hurry, I'd lose the dragon for sure.

"Are you looking for something?" Jules had obviously seen me look over at the park.

"Err—yes—err—I'm looking for Winky. I don't know where he's gone."

"The cat is in the office." Jules looked puzzled. "I saw him just before I left for the day."

"Really? Are you sure?"

"Positive. He was fast asleep on the sofa."

"Oh? That is good news. Well, I'd better not keep you both. Bye."

Jules kept looking back, as she walked away. She no doubt thought I'd lost my mind. Again!

As soon as they were out of sight, I hurried across the road, and found the nearest gate. Once inside the park, I managed to pick up the white trail. This park was much smaller than Washbridge Park, and there were very few people around. I followed the white trail until it came to a halt at a thick clump of bushes. A middle-aged woman was standing next to them, and she seemed quite distressed.

"Young lady!" She called to me. "Could you help me, please?"

"What seems to be the problem?"

"My dog, Brandy, has gone in there, and she won't come out."

I could hear a dog barking excitedly from somewhere inside the bushes.

"I think she must have seen something. Maybe a squirrel." The woman continued. "But I can't get to her—there are too many brambles."

She was right. I would have torn myself to pieces if I'd tried to push my way through.

"I'll go around the other side to see if it's any better," I said.

It wasn't, but I would have to get through the bushes somehow. I checked to make sure that the woman hadn't followed me, and that there was no one else around, then cast the 'shrink' spell. Now the size of a mouse, I scrambled through the undergrowth and eventually came to a clearing. Once there, I reversed the 'shrink' spell. The Jack Russell took no notice of me. She was too busy barking at the cotton dragon, which seemed totally unperturbed by the dog's presence. When the dog began to move towards it, the cotton dragon breathed a stream of fire, which sent the dog scuttling backwards. Fortunately, it appeared to be no more than a warning shot, which struck the ground a couple of feet in front of the dog. But, the stupid mutt didn't have the sense to run away. Instead, it began to move towards the dragon again. I was worried that the dragon's next shot might fry the dog. I had to act, and I had to act quickly, so I cast the 'rain' spell which made a small rain cloud appear above the cotton dragon. The short downfall soaked the dragon to the bone, and extinguished its flame. While the dragon was still stunned, I shrank it, and zipped it into my pocket.

Now, though, I had a problem. I needed to get the dog out, but I wouldn't be able to do that if I shrank myself. I had no option but to fight my way through the brambles while pulling the dog behind me by his collar.

"Brandy, there you are!" The woman grabbed the dog, and then turned to me. "Thank you so much. I'm so very grateful. Are you alright? Your arms and legs are scratched."

"I'm okay, thanks." I wasn't, but at least I had the cotton dragon.

I made my way back to Ever, where Grandma was waiting anxiously.

"Did you get it?" she said, as soon as I walked through the door.

"Yes," I took the tiny cotton dragon out of my pocket, and handed it to her.

"Good. I'll get it straight back to Candlefield." She looked me up and down. "And for goodness sake, tidy yourself up, Jill. You look like you've been pulled through a hedge backwards."

***

I couldn't go home looking like that. My arms and legs were a real mess, and my hair was full of twigs, leaves and goodness knows what else. Jack had sent me a message earlier to say he was already on his way home, so there was no chance of grabbing a shower and getting changed before he got in.

I always kept a change of clothes in the office—just in case of an emergency. I could use the showers at I-Sweat to get cleaned up. I'd still have the scratches, but provided I got rid of all the dried blood, Jack would probably never notice. You know how observant men are.

I hurried back to the office, collected my change of clothes, and then walked through to I-Sweat. I flashed my free pass at the young woman on reception, and made straight for the changing rooms.

The shower was just what the doctor ordered. By the time I came out, I felt completely refreshed. I quickly got dressed, and had just stepped out of the changing room when someone called to me.

"Jill?" It was Gavin, the instructor who had taken me through my paces on my first visit. "I didn't see you inside?"

"Err—no—I—was going to come in for a session, but then I got a phone call from home. I need to go."

He glanced at my wet hair.

"I got caught in a downpour earlier."

"Oh?" He looked understandably confused. The only rain in Washbridge that day had been from the cloud I'd magicked up to extinguish the dragon's flame. "Well, I hope it won't be long before we see you again, Jill."

"I'll do my best. Bye."

Gavin was a really good-looking guy, and unless I was

mistaken, he was sweet on me.

What? Who are you calling a sad, deluded fool?

***

When I walked into the house, I heard voices coming from the lounge. One of them was Jack, but I didn't recognise the other man's voice. There were no cars parked on the driveway, so who could it be?

The lounge door opened, and Jack appeared.

"Jill. Come and meet our new neighbour, Mr Kilbride."

To my horror, sitting on the sofa, was none other than the witchfinder. He gave me one of the creepiest smiles I'd ever seen in my life.

"Very pleased to meet you." He stood up and extended his hand. "Do call me Rory."

The man had an unusual accent, and mumbled badly. I could barely make out what he was saying.

"Sorry? I didn't quite catch your name."

"Rory."

I hesitated, but then shook his hand. His grip was exceedingly strong. So strong that it hurt my fingers, and caused me to pull away.

"I'm so sorry." He didn't look it. "I sometimes forget my own strength."

Why had Jack let this monster into the house? But of course, Jack had no idea that this man meant to kill me.

"I saw Rory standing on the front," Jack said. "So, I asked him over."

Great! "I assume you're not a local, Rory?"

"No. I've only just moved down here from Scotland for work."

"What do you do?"

"I'm in the occult business."

Occult? I felt a shiver run through my body. I just wanted this man out of my house. Fortunately, he must have read my mind.

"I can't stay." He started for the door. "I have important matters to attend to. Thank you again for the drink, Jack." He turned to me. "Very nice to meet you, Jill. I'm sure we'll see each other again soon. Very soon."

Jack showed him to the door.

"You were a bit cold with him, weren't you?" Jack said when he came back into the lounge.

"He gives me the creeps."

***

The nerve of the man. How dare Mr Rory Kilbride wheedle his way into my house, sit on my sofa, and drink my coffee, while all the time contemplating how he was going to kill me and Grandma. I had to put a stop to this, but first I would have to get hold of some Brewflower.

"We should have an early night," Jack suggested at nine-thirty.

"I'm always up for *an early night*." I flashed him my sexy smile.

What? I can do sexy when I want to.

"I meant so that we'd be refreshed for the big day, tomorrow."

Big day? Oh no! I'd blanked it out of my mind. The Washbridge social event of the year: Deli and Nails' wedding.

"Still if you're feeling frisky?" He grinned.

"I'm not now." The thought of the wedding had put a real damper on my ardour.

"So, are you coming up?"

"Not yet. I'll be up in a while."

"Okay." He gave me a peck on the lips, and then disappeared upstairs.

It was an hour later, after I'd seen the lights go out in the witchfinder's house, that I went to bed.

***

I woke suddenly, and sat up in bed. A noise had disturbed me, or had it been a dream? I checked the alarm clock; it was one o'clock. Jack was still fast asleep. Then, I heard it again. There was someone outside, at the front of the house.

I slipped quietly out of bed, threw on jeans and a T-shirt, and crept downstairs. I couldn't see anyone through the front window, so I listened again.

Footsteps!

It had to be the witchfinder—come to get me. My only chance was to get in first, and catch him off-guard. I had no idea what magic, if any, would work on him, but anything was better than sitting around, waiting for him to pounce.

I let myself quietly out of the front door. There were sounds coming from Megan's driveway—someone was standing behind her van—I could see their feet. This was it. It was him or me—a battle to the death.

"Kathy?"

She almost jumped out of her skin. "Jill? You scared me

to death."

"What are you doing here at this time of night," I said, in a whisper.

She had a paintbrush in one hand and a pot of white paint in the other.

"Nothing?" Kathy shrugged, all innocent like.

And then I saw it. Kathy had painted over Megan's picture on the side of the van.

"What have you done, Kathy? You'll get arrested."

"I don't care. She's now taken ten of Pete's customers, and he isn't doing anything about it. I'm not going to sit around and wait for her to take the rest of them." Kathy tried to pull away, but I kept hold of her arm.

"I'll have a word with Megan, and explain that she's affecting Peter's business. I'm sure once she's made aware of the situation, she'll stop."

"You have more faith in her than I do. I doubt she'll care."

"You have to at least give her a chance. If the police get involved, that will be even worse for Peter's business."

"It's too late now. It's already done."

"It isn't too late. I can still make this right."

"How? Look!" She pointed at her handiwork.

"Don't worry about that. I'll sort it." The 'take-it-back' spell would put it back to how it was, but I had to get rid of Kathy first. "Give me those." I snatched the paintbrush and paint tin from her. "Now get going before someone sees us."

"Okay. I'm sorry I woke you."

"Don't worry about it. Now go!"

I watched her walk away. Her car was parked a few doors down. As soon as she was inside it, I would cast the spell, and everything would be okay.

"Jill?"

"Megan? Hi."

She stared at the van, and then at the paintbrush and paint tin in my hands.

"I can explain. It isn't what it looks like."

Megan had disappeared into the house and slammed the door closed before I had chance to cast the 'forget' spell.

Oh bum!

Chapter 15

As soon as I woke up, I remembered what had happened the previous night. After Megan had rushed back into the house, I'd hung around in case she came out again, but she was obviously too freaked out. I'd half expected the police to come knocking at the door, but thankfully they hadn't. Yet.

How was I supposed to talk my way out of this one? There had been no point in using the 'take-it-back' spell because she'd already seen the damage. How would I ever make this right? What would I do if Megan told Jack? Or if the police came calling? Kathy had a lot to answer for.

And as if that wasn't bad enough, it was the day I'd been dreading for weeks: Deli and Nails' wedding. Why had we agreed to go? The answer to that was very simple: Jack had insisted on it because he wanted to meet more of my friends.

The guilty party was still asleep, so I slipped downstairs, and prepared a full English breakfast for him. Only when it was ready, did I call him to come down.

"Morning," he mumbled; his eyes were barely open. "Something smells nice."

"Take a seat before you fall down, Jack." I put his breakfast on the table in front of him.

"What's this?" He looked a little more awake now.

"What do you think it is? I've made breakfast for you." I joined him at the table.

"What have you done this time, Jill?" He took a bite of his sausage.

"What do you mean?"

"You've either done something, or you want something.

Why else would you have made me a full English?"

"Well, there's gratitude for you. I go to all the trouble of getting up early, and making you a full English breakfast, and you accuse me of ulterior motives."

"So, which is it? Have you done something, or do you want something?"

"Neither. And I'm disappointed that you would think that was my motive. But—"

"I knew it." He took a bite of the fried bread.

"I was just going to suggest that maybe we should give the wedding a miss?"

"I should have known. There had to be a reason for you to have gone to all this trouble."

"I don't know how you can even suggest that. The two things are totally unrelated."

"Don't give me that. You thought if you made breakfast for me that I'd agree to forget about the wedding, didn't you?"

"It's going to be terrible, Jack. You have no idea just how terrible."

"We've already accepted the invite, so we can hardly stay away now, can we?"

"Of course we can. They'll never notice if we don't turn up."

"We're going, and that's final."

I stood up. "You can wash the dishes!"

Two hours later, and I'd still been unable to convince Jack of the folly of attending this awful wedding. We were both dressed to the nines, waiting for the taxi to pick us up. I'd wanted to drive, but Jack had insisted we take a taxi so we could both have a drink. He was right; I was certainly going to need a few drinks to get me through the day.

"Have you got the present?" Jack asked.

"It's on the hallstand."

"I don't know why you insisted on buying this toaster." He picked up the present. "I still think the electric nail clippers would have been a much better gift."

"I'm not sure 'better' is the word I'd use. 'Creepy' is closer to the mark."

"I'm really looking forward to today." Jack gave me a peck on the cheek.

"Let's see if you still feel the same by the time we get home tonight."

Unfortunately, the taxi arrived on the dot. Jack and I climbed into the back.

"Register office, isn't it?" The driver had a pencil behind one ear, and a cigarette behind the other.

"That's right," Jack sounded altogether too chipper.

"You two getting hitched?"

"Not this time," Jack leant forward. "We're just guests."

Not this time? What did he mean by that?

A few minutes later, we pulled up at the toll bridge. When our driver wound down his window to pass over the money, I spotted Mr Ivers in the booth. Fortunately, he hadn't seen me, so I kept my head down.

It seemed to be taking an awfully long time to get going because five minutes later we were still stuck at the barrier.

"We've got a problem." The driver turned to us.

"What's up?" Jack asked.

"The barrier is stuck in the 'down' position. We can't get past."

Yes! I only just stopped myself from punching the air. "I suppose you'd better turn back, then," I suggested.

"Don't be ridiculous." Jack gave me a look. "If they can't get it working, we'll walk across the bridge, and call another taxi."

Sometimes Jack was way too smart for my liking.

"We might be here for a while," the driver said. "The funny little guy in the toll booth has sent for the maintenance crew.

Although I had no desire to go to the wedding, I had even less desire to hang around at the toll bridge because Mr Ivers was likely to spot me. The last thing I needed was to suffer his boring monologue on the latest movie releases.

I slipped out of the taxi, walked to the barrier, and quickly cast the 'power' spell. Once I'd done that, it was easy to lift the barrier clear of the car.

"Jill?" Mr Ivers shouted from the toll booth. "How did you manage that?"

"I didn't do anything. There must be a failsafe which kicks in in cases like this, so that the traffic isn't delayed. You'll still need your maintenance people to take a look at it, but at least the traffic will keep flowing."

Mr Ivers looked puzzled. At least I think he did; it was difficult to tell with him.

Back in the car, it was Jack's turn to give me a quizzical look.

"What?" I shrugged. "You wanted to get to the wedding, didn't you?"

We made it to the register office, but with only a few minutes to spare. It was just as well that we hadn't come in the car because the small car park was full, but not with cars. It was full of motorbikes and motor scooters.

"What are these doing here?" Jack asked me, as he paid the taxi driver.

"What do you think? They must belong to the guests."

"Surely not. No one comes to a wedding on a motorbike or scooter. Maybe there's some sort of bike-meet in town?"

Sometimes Jack was so naive it was painful.

That's when I spotted the 'yellow'. Mad was dressed from head to toe in it. She was wearing yellow high heels, yellow tights, a yellow dress and a tiny yellow hat, perched on top of her hair, which had been taken up into a bun.

"You can stop laughing, Jill." She came over to join us.

"You look really—err—yellow." I was desperately trying to curb the laughter, but it was proving to be impossible.

"I think you look very pretty," Jack said. "It's nice to see you again, and under better circumstances than the last time we met."

Jack and Mad had met before when he'd arrested her on suspicion of murdering the senior librarian.

"I'm sorry, Mad." I managed eventually. "It was just a bit of a shock."

"That's okay. I know what I look like. I'm never going to forgive my mum for this."

"Where's Henry?"

"He couldn't make it. He had a prior family commitment which was arranged long before Mum and

Nails set a date."

"Pity. I was hoping to meet him."

"The four of us should go out for dinner some time," Mad said.

"Sure, but only if you promise to wear your yellow ensemble?"

"No chance."

"We'd be up for dinner, wouldn't we, Jack?" I said.

"Yes. Definitely."

Suddenly, something seemed to distract Mad. She was staring at the register office.

"Are you okay, Mad?"

"Could I have a quick word, Jill, please?" She grabbed my arm, and pulled me to one side.

"What's wrong?"

"Over there—at the corner of the building. There's a ghost. I thought I spotted him earlier."

"Who is it? Do you know?"

"Yeah. It's Tommy Cinders. He's an old boyfriend of Mum's. He and she were seeing one another when he died in a tragic accident. He was trampled to death by an elephant, which had escaped from a travelling circus."

"That's horrible." I shuddered at the thought. "Why do you think he's here?"

"To stop Mum marrying Nails. I've come across Tommy's ghost before, and he told me that he didn't want Mum seeing anyone else. I usually just ignore him, but I'm worried he might cause trouble today. Can you hold onto these flowers while I go and sort him out?"

"Sure."

After I'd taken the bouquet from her, Mad went

charging towards the register office.

"What's going on?" Jack asked. "Is your friend okay?"

"Yeah, I think so. She's just got a touch of yellow fever."

I laughed at my own joke. Someone had to.

Before Jack could press me for more information, the roar of a huge engine drowned out our conversation. A monster truck, with wheels as tall as me, pulled up in front of the register office gates. The passenger door opened, and out climbed Nails; he was dressed as a teddy boy: purple drape coat, purple drainpipe trousers, and purple brothel creepers. His hair was slicked back with Brylcreem, or maybe it was lard.

Nails leapt down from the truck, and was soon joined by the driver. He too was dressed in teddy boy attire, blue being his colour of choice. The two of them hurried past us into the register office.

"We should probably go inside," Jack said.

"There's still time to do a runner." I was clutching at straws.

Jack grabbed my arm, and led me inside. The room was full of bikers, mods and teddy boys. I'd never seen a crowd quite like it. We managed to find two free seats on the second row from the back. I was seated next to a biker who was wearing a leather jacket with a skull and crossbones painted on the back.

"I've arrested half of the people in here," Jack whispered.

"Don't blame me. I did warn you."

I almost jumped out of my skin when heavy metal music began to belt through the speakers; it was deafening. Jack and I exchanged a glance, and I mouthed the words: '*I warned you*'.

No one else seemed concerned by the volume of the music; in fact, several people began to dance. Moments later, Deli appeared in the doorway behind us. The music stopped, and all heads turned to look at her.

She was wearing the shortest red dress I'd ever seen. One wrong move, and she would be flashing her panties for all to see. The neckline plunged so low I could see her navel. Her red heels were so high that she struggled to walk to the front of the room where Nails was waiting for her to join him. Just then, a breathless Mad came charging in. She'd lost her hat, and her face was flushed. As she passed by me, she gave me a thumbs up, and grabbed the bouquet of flowers.

The ceremony itself was something of a blur. Both Nails and Deli had written their own vows, and to say they were nonsensical would have been an understatement. There was even mention of a dress allowance and cigarette money.

When the ceremony was finally over, we all made our way into the gardens at the rear of the building. The borders were resplendent with flowers, but no amount of flowers could salvage this train wreck of a wedding.

Jack and I found a quiet spot in one corner of the garden, but we still got dragged into a few group photos. I noticed some of the guests do a double take when they saw Jack. They were probably trying to recall where they knew him from. Hopefully they wouldn't remember it was when he had handcuffed them.

Eventually all the photographs had been taken, and we all made our way to the front of the building where a double-decker bus was waiting for us. Nails had hired it to take everyone to the reception, which was being held in a pub a couple of miles down the road. Jack and I sat downstairs at the very front. I figured that would give us the best chance of a quick escape if the assembled crowd remembered how they knew Jack.

The bus pulled up outside a pub called 'Rough and Ready'; a very apt name, if ever there was one. Mad led the way inside. If I'd thought it looked bad from the outside that was nothing to the delights awaiting us inside. It was a real 'spit and sawdust' establishment, which hadn't seen a lick of paint since the turn-of-the-century. The nineteenth century.

The lighting wasn't so much subdued as broken. Every other bulb was either blown or missing. At least that meant we couldn't see the carpet which was so sticky that it felt like it was trying to suck us under. There were all manner of stains on the walls and furniture—I really did not want to know what they were.

"Help yourself to food, everyone!" Deli was standing arm in arm with her new husband, who was busy picking at a hangnail.

Four large tables had been pushed together to accommodate the food. And a motley spread it was too. There were chips, and sausages, and more chips, and pickled eggs, and more chips, and sandwiches made on bread so thick it would have broken your toe if you'd dropped it. And did I mention beer? There was lots of that, too.

But not for very long.

The bikers, mods and teddy boys alike, descended on the spread, like wolves on a carcass. Within minutes, every plate and dish had been stripped bare, and there wasn't a bottle of beer to be had.

"Good thing we weren't hungry," Jack quipped.

Once the tables had been cleared away, the music started up. It was an eclectic mix of heavy metal, rock and roll and punk—all of it pre-1980. The guests, all now well lubricated, descended on the space where the tables had been. There was barely enough room to accommodate all the dancers (and I use that term very loosely). Every now and then, a scuffle would break out between the different factions: teddy boys, mods and bikers.

Thankfully, Jack and I managed to find a relatively quiet corner where we could at least hear ourselves think, if not speak. The next two hours lasted an eternity. Then, for a moment, I thought I'd gone deaf, but realised that the music had been turned off to enable Nails to announce that he and his new bride were leaving to go on honeymoon to an undisclosed destination on the south coast. Everyone came out of the pub to bid them farewell as they rode away on a huge chopper-style motorbike. Deli was up front; Nails was riding pillion.

Once they'd disappeared into the distance, everyone else piled back into the pub, but I grabbed Jack's arm, and pulled him back.

"I can't stand another minute. Let's go home."

"But no one else has left yet. Won't it look rude?"

"Who cares?"

"What about Mad?"

"I haven't seen anything of the canary since we came to the pub. I reckon she's already made her getaway. Come on, we're going." I hailed a cab.

It was so good to get back home. Jack made coffee, and we both collapsed onto the sofa.

"Well." Jack took a sip of his coffee. "That was certainly different."

"I did try to warn you." I sighed. "No more weddings for me."

"Are you sure about that? Not even one more?"

Chapter 16

I'd spoken to Lily Padd who, like Mrs Rollo, had had her savings snatched by the scam artist who was peddling non-existent timeshare holidays. The other woman that I'd tried to contact via the Merry Widows forum had never got back to me. So far, I was no nearer to tracking the conman down. Sometimes, though, I was guilty of not being able to see the wood for the trees, and maybe this was one of those times. There was something I needed to check with Mrs Rollo, so I called at her house on my way out to work.

"Jill? Good morning. Aren't you at work today?"

"Yes, I'm on my way there now, but I wondered if I could have a quick word with you, first?"

"Of course. Do come in."

"I can only stay for a moment."

"Long enough to pick out a bun to take to work with you, surely?"

Oh, dear.

I followed her into the kitchen.

"I suppose you heard I was eliminated from the Big Bake Challenge?"

"I had no idea."

Mrs Rollo had got through the first round of the Big Bake Challenge courtesy of a little magic provided by yours truly.

"I didn't realise that they'd recorded the second round."

"It was last week. I would have asked you to come along, but my cousins were desperate for tickets. I hope you don't mind?"

Mind? I couldn't have been any more relieved.

"Not at all. How did it go?"

"Not very well, unfortunately. In fact, I came last. I think I must have misjudged the ingredients. It was a bit of a disaster."

"I must say, Mrs Rollo. You seem to be taking it very well?"

"There aren't many people who get invited to take part in that competition, and fewer still who get through the first round. So, all in all, I'm proud of what I achieved."

"And so you should be. What did your cousins make of it?"

"They still enjoyed themselves even though I didn't do very well on the night. Now, Jill, what was it you wanted to talk to me about?"

"Have you by any chance ever posted on a forum called the Merry Widows of Washbridge?"

"Yes, I have. I don't really go in for the internet, but one of my friends introduced me to the Merry Widows forum, and I do go on there from time to time."

"Do you mind if I ask what name you post under?"

"Master Baker."

Of course she did.

"Tell me, did you post about the conman?"

"No. I was too embarrassed. Why are you interested in the Merry Widows forum, Jill?"

"Just a hunch that I'm working on. It may turn out to be nothing."

"I see." She pointed at the table which was full of buns, or at least I think that's what they were meant to be. If ever someone needed to reimagine baking, it was Mrs Rollo. "Which one would you like to take with you?"

It was a difficult choice. Not because they were all so

appetising, but because I had zero idea what any of them was. In the end, I chose a pink one. Surely, that had to be strawberry?

"Good choice, Jill. I call that one lemon surprise."

***

I'd arranged to meet with the NOCA committee at Chuckle House to give them feedback on my investigation to date—such as it was. The day of the clown convention was looming, and a decision had to be made as to whether to go ahead with it or not. In attendance, as per the previous meeting, were: Andrew Clowne, Don Keigh, and Ray Carter.

Andrew Clowne chaired the meeting. "I think we should begin by asking Jill what progress she's made in finding the would-be extortionist."

All eyes were now on me.

"I'm afraid I haven't made much headway. I've been unable to identify who is behind the threat."

"That's very disappointing," Andrew Clowne said. "I had hoped that the perpetrator would have been in custody by now. But, as that's not the case, then regrettably I must change my position in regard to the upcoming conference."

"Change your position how?" Ray Carter asked.

"As you know, I wasn't in favour of paying the extortion demand, but now I don't see that we have any choice if we still plan to go ahead with the conference."

"Don't be ridiculous." Don Keigh thumped the table. "Why should we pay? I'm still convinced this whole thing is a hoax."

"I don't agree with paying either," Ray Carter said. "I'm still of the opinion that we should bring in the police."

"Do you two really want to take the risk of this blowing up in our faces?" Andrew Clowne looked from one man to the other. "If we don't pay, and this man carries out his threats, how do you think that will make us look?"

"Just a second," I interrupted. "I think paying the money would be a mistake. Like Don, I too believe that this is little more than a hoax."

"What about the two murders?" Andrew Clowne turned his gaze on me.

"I've spoken to a number of people concerning the two deaths referred to in the extortion letter, and I'm now convinced that neither of those was murder. It's clear to me that they were in fact both the result of tragic accidents, which could have been avoided. I don't believe the person who wrote the letter had anything to do with those deaths at all. It's my opinion that he's simply trying to scare you into giving in to his demands."

"So what are you saying, Jill?" Don Keigh said. "Do you think we're okay to go ahead with the conference?"

"I do. I would recommend proceeding with the conference as planned."

There was further discussion during which Andrew Clowne continued to push for the payment to be made. When it came to the vote, the committee voted two-to-one to proceed with the conference, but not to make any payment to the extortionist. Andrew Clowne was clearly unhappy with the result, which was a little surprising because when he'd first come to my office, he'd been totally against making a payment to the extortionist.

***

As I made my way back to the office, I was forced to make a detour because Lombard Road had been cordoned off. The police were stopping anyone driving or even walking down the street.

When I eventually arrived at the office, Mrs V was at her desk, talking to Gavin, the instructor from I-Sweat.

"Hello, you two."

"Morning, Jill," Mrs V said. "I've been for another session next door. Gavin thinks I'm improving, don't you Gavin?"

"Definitely, Mrs V. You put a lot of women half your age to shame."

Mrs V beamed.

"Anyway, I'd better get back." Gavin started for the door. "I hope we'll see you around there again soon, Jill."

"I'll do my best."

"What a nice young man," Mrs V said, after he had left.

"Very good looking too."

"Jill!"

"What? I'm only saying. Anyway, do you know what's going on with the police roadblocks in town?"

"There's been a bank robbery. Haven't you heard?"

"I've been in a meeting; I haven't heard the news this morning."

I went through to my office where Winky was sitting cross-legged on the sofa. His eyes were shut, and he was chanting quietly. I knew I was going to regret asking, but curiosity got the better of me.

"What are you doing, Winky?"

"Do you mind? I'm trying to meditate."

"Since when did you meditate?"

"Since I rejected this material world in favour of a more spiritual existence."

"Really? This was all kind of sudden, wasn't it?"

"Inner peace is more important to me now than possessions or relationships."

"I see. And how long do you think this will last?"

"This is now my life's focus."

"Okay. Well, good luck with that."

He went back to his chanting.

I brought up the local news on my web browser. As expected, the headline story was the robbery of Washbridge Central Bank. I made a call.

"Blaze, I assume you've seen the news?"

"Yeah. It has all the hallmarks of Slippery Sam. I'm as good as dead. Daze will kill me when she gets back."

"Maybe you'll find him before she does."

"I doubt it. He'll be long gone by now."

I felt sorry for Blaze. He'd been so looking forward to having more responsibility while Daze was away, but it had all gone pear-shaped for him.

***

"Do you have to make that noise all the time?" I said.

"Please don't refer to it as *noise*." Winky gave me a one-eyed look. "It's my mantra, and yes, I do have to chant it all the time. How else will I find inner peace?"

"Could you at least chant a little more quietly? I'm trying to pick out a new pair of shoes here."

There was a sale on at Vintage-Shoes-4-U, and I couldn't decide which of two pairs I liked best.

"You spend too much time worrying about materialistic things, Jill. It's time you began to think more about your spiritual well-being, and became one with the universe."

Just then, something caught my eye across the way.

"So let me get this straight," I said. "You're no longer interested in possessions or relationships? Is that right?"

"Precisely."

"In that case, you won't care that the cat who has moved in across the way appears to have mastered semaphore?"

Winky stopped chanting, jumped into the windowsill, grabbed his little flags, and began to wave them frantically. While Winky was busy conversing via semaphore with his new girlfriend, I logged onto the Merry Widows forum, and searched for posts by 'Master Baker'. There were quite a few, but the one that caught my eye had been posted in the 'holidays' section. Master Baker, a.k.a. Mrs Rollo, had posted at length about her love of holidays, and her desire to holiday with her children and grandchildren. The post was dated only a few days prior to the conman appearing at her door.

It now seemed obvious that the conman had targeted his victims based upon posts they had made on that forum. If my suspicions were correct, perhaps I could ensnare him by posting a similar message. But first, I needed to add a postal address to my profile. I entered Kathy's address because, if my suspicions were correct, the conman was hardly likely to target a house next door to one he'd already scammed. I'd just have to make sure that I warned Kathy about what I'd done in case anyone contacted her. I then made a post in the holidays section in which I mentioned my love of holidays, particularly in

Spain. I also mentioned how much I loved to holiday with my kids and grandkids. Hopefully, that would be bait enough to attract our friend, the conman. We'd see.

***

Winky was busy with the semaphore for almost an hour. When he finally put down the little flags, and jumped out of the windowsill, he looked exceedingly pleased with himself.

"What's your new girlfriend's name?"

"Peggy." He jumped onto my desk. "She's a real little hottie."

"I despair of you sometimes."

"She *is* hot. And, she's obviously taken a shine to me. She spent all day and night learning semaphore just so we could communicate."

"Where does this leave Bella?"

"Who?" Winky shrugged. "She's history now—her and her deportment classes. Peggy says that I'm the most handsome cat she's seen since she moved into the neighbourhood."

"I take it she's a house cat then?"

"Cheek!"

"What about the meditation, the chanting, and the renouncement of material goods and relationships? What about being one with the universe?"

"Stuff the universe. I'm so over that."

So fickle.

Chapter 17

Jack pulled onto the drive just ahead of me. As I got out of my car, I saw Megan come out of her front door. Oh no! This could be very awkward.

"Hi!" Jack called to her. "I see you have new artwork on your van."

"Yes." Megan glared at me. "I had to get it re-done."

Instead of the large image of herself, the van now displayed a picture of a lawn with flowered borders.

"I like it." Jack nodded his approval. "What do you think, Jill?"

Megan was still glaring at me.

"I think it's really nice." Any moment now, Megan would tell Jack why she'd been forced to make the change. "Come on, Jack." I grabbed his arm. "We'd better get in. I'm sure Megan's very busy."

Before he had the chance to argue, I'd dragged him inside.

"What's up?" He looked nonplussed.

"What do you mean?"

"Have you and Megan fallen out?"

"No. What makes you think that?"

"The way she was glaring at you out there. If looks could kill, you'd be a goner."

"I don't know what you mean. She seemed okay to me."

"So why did you drag me inside?"

"Because I had other plans." I grabbed his hand, and led him up the stairs. "Come with me."

That brought a smile to his face.

The sacrifices I had to make.

Later, much later, when we were eating dinner, I was still wondering how I could put things right with Megan. At least she hadn't said anything to Jack—not yet. What would he think if she did? That he was living with a mad woman? Probably.

"Jill? Did you hear what I said?" Jack nudged me.

I hadn't. I'd been miles away. "Sorry?"

"I said that I found out today that I have to work a case with Leo Riley."

"Which case?"

"Did you hear that there'd been a bank robbery in Washbridge?"

"Yeah. I had to take a diversion because the road was closed."

"There was also a bank robbery in West Chipping a couple of days earlier. The powers-that-be think that the two robberies are connected, so they want me and Leo Riley to team up. That should be fun; the man can barely bring himself to speak to me."

"If you'd like me to mediate, you can always give me a call."

"Not helpful, Jill."

***

The next morning, Jack had to leave the house early because he'd arranged to meet Leo Riley. To say that Jack wasn't a happy bunny would have been an understatement. I'd told him that he should learn to rub along better with people.

What do you mean that's rich coming from me?

I made a call to Blaze.

"Have you heard from Daze?"

"No, thank goodness. I'm dreading her coming back. She's going to kill me."

"I thought I'd better let you know that the police are linking the bank robbery in Washbridge with one in West Chipping. The two forces are working together on this now."

"They're barking up the wrong tree. Slippery Sam didn't rob the bank in West Chipping; I can guarantee that. And besides, he's long gone now."

***

When I walked into the office, Winky was sitting on the windowsill, little flags in hand. He didn't acknowledge me; he was too busy semaphoring sweet nothings to his new girlfriend.

By the time I'd checked my emails, and looked through the morning's post, Winky had jumped down from the windowsill, and was resting on the sofa. Semaphore was clearly hard work.

"I take it your new love interest is working out okay?"

"Couldn't be better. In fact, I've invited Peggy over here for dinner."

"And, of course, you were going to ask me if that was okay?"

"It'll be one evening after you've finished for the day. And don't worry, I'll make all the arrangements—organise the food etc. You won't need to do anything."

"Good to know."

The next thing I knew, Winky had jumped off the sofa,

and crawled underneath it. Before I could ask him what was wrong, I had my answer. The temperature in the room fell dramatically, and moments later, the colonel appeared. He looked much happier than the last time he'd paid me a visit.

Before I'd even had a chance to greet him, he'd taken me into his arms, and given me a ghostly hug. It's difficult to know how to describe being hugged by a ghost—it's kind of weird.

"I don't know how I'll ever be able to thank you, Jill." The colonel eventually released me, and took a step back.

"It's nice to see you smiling again, Colonel."

"However did you do it?"

"I take it we're talking about the house?"

"Sorry, I should have said. Yes, the property developer has been outbid. My beautiful house now belongs to a man with an unusual name. But then, you already know that, I assume?"

"I was hoping that Murray Murray would put in an offer for the house. He certainly seemed quite keen when I told him about it."

"I believe he's in the music business?"

"A pop sensation, apparently."

"Sorry?"

"Just my little joke. Yes, he's very successful."

"How do you know him?"

"I don't really. I helped him to recover his watch and wallet. We got talking, and he mentioned that he liked this area of the country, but had been unable to find a suitable property to buy. I told him about your house, and he seemed very interested. I'm glad it's worked out for both of you."

"It certainly has. The thought of the house being demolished was simply too much to bear, but now it looks as though a whole new generation will be able to enjoy it. And, of course, it means that Cilla and I will be able to continue to live there."

"Where is Cilla, anyway?"

"She's come down with the flu, so I told her to stay in bed."

"Oh dear. Tell her I hope she feels better soon."

"I will, and thanks again, Jill. For everything."

No sooner had the colonel taken his leave than my phone rang. It was Kathy.

"Jill? Do you know anything about timeshares?"

Oh bum! I hadn't gotten around to telling her that I'd used her address on the Merry Widows forum.

"Not really. Why?"

"The strangest thing just happened. Just after Pete left, a weird man came to the door. He asked to speak to Kathy. I said that I was Kathy, which seemed to throw him a little, but then he went on to ask if I liked to holiday with my children and grandchildren. Grandchildren? Cheek of the man! I asked him if I looked old enough to have grandchildren. Then he tried to sell me some kind of timeshare, so I sent him away with a flea in his ear."

"That does sound rather strange." It was too late now to explain about the forum — better to play dumb. "What did he look like?"

"Why?"

"No reason. Just curious."

"He was bald. Probably in his early sixties. And he smelled like pork chops."

"Nice. Anyway, while you're on. I have a bone to pick with you."

"What have I done this time?"

"You've dropped me right in it with Megan."

"How come?"

"A few seconds after you disappeared the other night, she came out of the house, and caught me holding the paintbrush and paint tin. She thinks *I* was responsible for painting over her van."

Kathy laughed.

"It's not funny. She isn't speaking to me now."

"I'm sorry, Jill. I didn't mean to get you into trouble. What are you going to do about it?"

"I don't know. I'll probably tell her that I was sleepwalking."

"With paint and a paint brush?"

"Have you got any better ideas?"

"Not really. Has she said anything to Jack?"

"Not yet, thank goodness. But I'm worried she might be biding her time. She's already had the van repainted. It's much more tasteful now. She's got rid of the picture of herself, and replaced it with a picture of a lawn and flowerbed."

"Good. Maybe she won't be able to poach as many of Pete's customers now."

I'd no sooner finished talking to Kathy than my phone rang again.

"Aunt Lucy? Is everything okay over there?"

"Yes. Everything is fine. Well, I say fine, but there is something that I need to talk to you about, and it would be better if you could come over so we can do it face to face."

"When?"

"Now if possible. I've asked the twins to come over too. Something has cropped up out of the blue, and I think we all need to talk about it to decide what we're going to do."

"Sure. I'll come right over."

I arrived outside Aunt Lucy's house at the same time as the twins.

"I take it that you've been summoned too, Jill?" Amber said.

"Yeah. Aunt Lucy rang me a couple of minutes ago. She said something had cropped up, but she didn't say what. Do you two know what it's all about?"

"No idea." Pearl shrugged. "She wouldn't tell us on the phone. I hope she hasn't dragged us out here just to have another moan about Lester."

"Let's find out." I pushed open the door, and the twins followed me inside.

Aunt Lucy was in the kitchen; she already had the kettle on. On the kitchen table was a plate of cupcakes, and the Tupperware box containing my custard creams.

What? Of course they were *my* custard creams. Let anyone else try to pinch one if they dared.

"Thanks for coming over, everyone." Aunt Lucy greeted us with a huge smile—that was reassuring, at least. If it had been anything serious, she would have looked much more concerned.

"Help yourselves to cakes." Aunt Lucy turned around. "Oh? I see you two already have."

The twins were already munching on cupcakes. I, of course, had been much more restrained, and was only on my second custard cream.

"Tea or coffee?" Aunt Lucy asked.

"Tea for me, please," I said.

The twins elected to have tea, too.

Aunt Lucy joined us at the table. "Right girls. It seems that Grandma has decided it will be her birthday in three days' time."

The twins and I exchanged glances.

"What do you mean 'decided'?" I asked. "Surely, your birthday is on the anniversary of the day you were born. You don't get to decide when it is."

"That's right," Amber said, through a mouthful of strawberry cupcake.

"It would be great if you did get to choose when your birthday is." Pearl picked up a second cupcake. "I'd have one every month. Just think of all those presents."

"Your grandmother doesn't celebrate her birthday very often," Aunt Lucy said. "So, she reckons that gives her licence to decide when she will have one, and she has decided that it will be in three days' time. She informed me of this late last night, and also told me that she'd like a party and lots of presents."

"That woman is unbelievable!" I said, then looked around to make sure she hadn't crept in without me hearing her.

"That may be so." Aunt Lucy sighed. "But she's made her mind up, and I doubt we're going to change it. The problem is it's too late to book anywhere at such short notice. I've called all the usual places, and they're all booked up, so we'll have to have the party here."

"Who are we going to invite?" I asked. "What about her poker buddies?"

"She said it should be family only, so it looks like it will be the four of us plus Alan, William, and Lester."

Little did Jack know how lucky he was to have escaped this nightmare.

"I'll prepare all the food," Aunt Lucy said. "And you two." She pointed to the twins. "You are responsible for getting all the balloons, party poppers, party hats and whatever else we need for a party."

"What about presents?" I asked.

"It's up to each of you to buy a present, and heaven help you if you get it wrong."

Chapter 18

What did you buy for the woman who'd had centuries to accumulate everything? I had no idea, but I knew one thing for sure. If I got it wrong, I'd never hear the end of it. I'd racked my brains, and so far, had come up with nothing. But then it occurred to me that Kathy spent way more time with Grandma than I did. Maybe she'd heard her mention something that she would like. It was worth a shot.

When I walked into Ever A Wool Moment, I was surprised to find someone else behind the counter. Chloe, that was the name on her badge, was helping a customer to sign up for Everlasting Wool. I waited until she had finished.

"Are you new here, Chloe?"

"I'm a temp. I'm only here for a few weeks. Is there something I can help you with? Are you interested in signing up for an Everlasting Wool subscription?"

"No, thanks. I'm Kathy's sister. You don't know where she is, do you?"

"She's up on the new roof terrace." Chloe pointed. "You need to take the stairs."

"Thanks."

I made my way up the stairs. It had been quite cold outside, and I assumed it would be even colder on the roof. But, when I stepped out onto the terrace, I found myself in bright sunshine. It didn't make any sense. When I'd walked down the high street, the sky had been overcast and grey, and there had been a cool breeze. But up there, the air was still, and it was hot. So hot in fact that I had to take off my coat.

The roof had been transformed. Artificial grass covered the floor, and pot plants were scattered around the perimeter. The terrace was buzzing with people all dressed as though it was the height of summer. Some were in summer dresses, others in shorts and T-shirts. One woman was even sporting a bathing costume. The majority of them were sitting on deck chairs and sun loungers. Some were sipping cold drinks through straws—others were busy knitting.

Kathy was carrying a tray, offering the customers a selection of cold drinks. I eventually managed to catch her eye, and she came over.

"I didn't sign up to be a waitress," she complained.

"How come you aren't working downstairs?"

"That's what I'd like to know. I assumed when your grandmother brought in a temp, the temp would be up here serving drinks."

"How come she isn't?"

"Your grandmother said she wanted me to take charge of this new venture."

"Where is Grandma anyway?"

"That's a good question. She's left muggins here holding the fort, as usual."

"How come it's so hot up here?"

"Don't ask me." Kathy shrugged. "Your grandmother did try to explain it. Something about geophysics, science, and weather systems. She had me blinded with science."

"It seems very popular."

"No kidding. I haven't stopped since I came up here. I'm just hoping nobody has one too many drinks, and forgets we're on the roof. It's quite a fall from up here. What brings you around here, anyway?"

"I wanted to pick your brain. I have to get a birthday present for Grandma. I need to buy something in time for the party."

"Party?" Kathy was furious. "Nobody's invited me to a party!"

Oh bum!

What an idiot I was. Why had I mentioned the party? There was no good way to explain why she hadn't been invited. I had no choice but to cast the 'forget' spell, and get out of there as quickly as I could. I'd just have to work out what to buy Grandma by myself.

***

As I walked back along the high street, I was still thinking about what I could buy Grandma for her birthday. I had very little time to come up with something, and if I didn't get it right, I would be in deep doo doo.

On the other side of the road, a few doors up from Betty's shop, another new shop had opened. Those particular premises had been boarded-up for some time—ever since the sewing machine repair shop had closed several months earlier. The Final Straw sold fruit drinks, and made the unlikely claim of having one million flavours to choose from.

I popped across the road to check it out. Inside, the shop looked as though a rainbow had just exploded. Every table and chair was a different colour. One of the walls was yellow, another was blue, another green and the other one was red. The ceiling and floor were both pink.

I was quite thirsty, so decided I'd give it a try.

A young woman, wearing a multi-coloured T-shirt and cap, came skipping over.

"Hi, I'm Gina. Is this your first time in The Final Straw?"

"Yes. What flavours do you have?"

Gina pointed to the small tablets mounted on the counter. She twirled one around so we could both see the screen.

"The flavours are listed in alphabetical order. You can have a single flavour for two pounds, or three flavours for three pounds, or five flavours for four pounds. Which would you like?"

"I'll go for the three flavours, please."

I wasn't convinced there were actually a million different flavours listed, but there were certainly a lot to choose from. In the end, I chose Pineapple Surprise for my first flavour, Passionfruit Supreme for my second, and Mango Max for my third.

Gina took my money and then walked away. I waited for a couple of minutes, but she showed no sign of bringing my drink.

"Excuse me?" I called to her.

"Yes?"

"I was wondering where my drink was?"

"Oh sorry. I'd forgotten this was your first time. The information is all on here." She took the receipt back from me. "Look, it's printed there on the bottom. Table: three. Straw number: 1814."

"Sorry, I still don't understand how it works."

"Table three is the green one over there in the corner. If you take a seat there, your drink will be with you shortly."

This was all very confusing, but I did as she said, and sat at table number three. But I still had no drink. Then suddenly a small circular section in the centre of the table slid to one side. Moments later, a straw came up through the hole, and began to slide towards me. There was a small tag attached to the straw — it read: order 1814.

I took a sip. It didn't taste much like pineapple, passionfruit or mango. It tasted more like flat cola. I glanced around at the other tables; everyone was drinking from similar straws. It was certainly a novel approach, and presumably saved on the washing up.

I checked the local news on my phone. The headline story was about a man who'd been found murdered in his home. Percival Berry was a retired civil servant and, according to the article, an amateur clown known as Mr Bobo.

I'd no sooner finished reading the news article than my phone rang.

"Have you seen the news about Mr Bobo, Jill?" Andrew Clowne said.

"Yes. I've just this minute read it."

"Are you able to come over for an emergency meeting? I've already spoken to Don and Ray. They can be here in thirty minutes."

"At Chuckle House?"

"Yeah."

"Okay. I'll be there as soon as I can."

I'd had quite enough of my pineapple/passionfruit/mango concoction. On the way out, I stopped at table seven, which was closest to the door. The young man sitting there was sucking on a straw while playing Angry Birds on his phone. I tapped him on the shoulder to get his attention.

"Sorry to disturb you."

"Yeah?" He looked a little disgruntled at having been interrupted mid-game.

"I just wondered. What flavours did you order?"

"Banana Breeze, Apple Action and Plum Passion."

"And what do you think of it?"

"It tastes like flat cola to me."

Hmmm.

***

The three men were already seated when I arrived at the meeting. The atmosphere was sombre, as was to be expected given the recent turn of events.

"Gentlemen, and Jill." Andrew Clowne was chairing the meeting as usual. "I'm sure we can all agree that the events of yesterday evening are nothing short of a tragedy. The three of us all knew Mr Bobo. His death is a loss not only to his family but to the whole clown community. I must also report to the meeting that I have received another note from the extortionist." He took a sheet of paper from his pocket, and held it out. The words had been produced using cuttings from newspapers as had the previous note. He read the letter aloud, "Ignore this final demand at your peril. You will know by now that I am deadly serious. Unless the money is delivered tomorrow, two more people will die during the upcoming conference."

Everyone took a moment to take it in, but then Andrew Clowne continued, "As you all know, I had been totally against paying the money, but I don't see how we can ignore this now. Whoever is behind this, is obviously deranged, but deadly serious. We have to take another vote right now to decide what we're going to do. The question before us is a simple one: Do we pay the money? I vote yes."

Ray was next to speak. "I don't think the money should be paid. You simply cannot give in to people like this. But the conference must be cancelled. We cannot possibly carry on after what has happened to Mr Bobo. I vote no."

"You know that I thought this was a hoax all along," Don Keigh said. "But I've been proven wrong. However, this conference has been running for almost a hundred years, and has never been cancelled—not even during the war. I do not want to be on the committee that cancels this for the first time in its history. It's for that reason, and that reason only, that I vote yes. We should pay the money."

"That's decided then," Andrew Clowne said. "The motion is passed two votes to one."

"How do we pay the money?" Don Keigh asked.

"This latest note says we'll get further instructions tomorrow, but we can decide who'll make the drop now. I think I should do it."

"No," I said. "You hired me to stop this man. I haven't been able to do that, but I won't stand idly by while one of you gets hurt. We have no idea what this man is capable of. I'm better placed to deal with someone like this than any of you. I should take the money."

"I agree," Ray Carter said.

Don Keigh nodded.

"Okay," Andrew Clowne said. "In that case, once I have the final instructions tomorrow, I'll get in touch with you, Jill. In the meantime, I'll withdraw the money from the bank, and have it ready."

***

After I'd finished at Chuckle House, I decided not to go into the office. I wanted to get home before Jack because there was something important I had to do. Something I wasn't looking forward to at all.

Megan's van was on her driveway. A part of me had hoped that it wouldn't be—that would have given me a get out. But, I knew it was time for me to try to put things right.

When I knocked on her door, she glanced out of the window. I waved, but she just shook her head. Who could blame her? Why would she answer the door to the mad paint woman?

I mouthed the word 'please'.

She thought about it for a while, and then came to the door. "What do you want, Jill? I have nothing to say to you."

"Can I come in, please?"

"Why? Do you want to scribble all over my walls with a pen?"

"I know I deserve that, but if you'd just let me in for a couple of minutes, I can explain."

Megan stood to one side, and allowed me in, but she didn't invite me into the lounge. Instead we stood and talked in the hallway.

"What do you want to say to me?" She was as icy as it was possible to be.

"I'm so sorry about what I did. I've been having a lot of trouble sleeping lately, so I went to see the doctor. He prescribed sleeping pills, but they obviously didn't agree with me because I started sleepwalking. That's what happened that night. I wasn't awake; I was just sleepwalking."

"Why did you paint over my van?"

"While I was sleepwalking, I was having a dream about a pink elephant which asked me to paint it white."

What? I'd like to see you come up with something better.

"A pink elephant asked you to paint it white?" Megan's expression was one of total confusion.

"I know it sounds crazy, but it was all down to the sleeping pills. I've stopped taking them now, obviously, but I feel terrible about what I did that night. I value our friendship, and I'm hoping you can find it in your heart to forgive me."

And the Oscar goes to…

She thought about it for the longest moment, but then managed a weak smile. "That must have been terrible for you, Jill? You must have been terrified when you woke up?"

"I was, and horrified at what I'd done."

"It obviously wasn't your fault."

"I still feel responsible. I hope you will at least allow me to pay for the work you've had done on the van."

"Okay. If you're sure."

I was sure—sure that Kathy would be picking up that particular bill.

"Definitely. And, why don't you come over and have dinner with Jack and me one night?"

"I'd like that, thanks. Would it be okay if I brought my new boyfriend with me?"

"Of course, the more, the merrier."

Chapter 19

Jack was already eating breakfast when I got up. I'd slept much better for having resolved the issue with Megan, and there hadn't been a single elephant in my dreams: white or pink.

"What time did you get in last night?" I asked, as I slid two slices of bread into the toaster.

"Just after midnight. Leo Riley is driving me insane; the man's an idiot. He's being deliberately obstructive at every turn. The sooner this case is sorted, the better I'll like it."

"Do you want another drink?"

"No, I have to get off. I'm working out of Washbridge again today."

"No progress on the bank robberies so far, then?"

"Not really. I have my doubts that the two robberies are connected. The only thing they have in common is that they were both committed at night. Whoever hit the West Chipping bank used industrial tools to remove the ATMs. Their escape was caught on CCTV—they were in a white van with false number plates. These guys actually took the ATMs away with them."

"What about the Washbridge robbery."

"That's just it. There's no indication of how the robbers got into the bank, and no sign of them making their escape. It's like the money disappeared into fresh air. We have no idea who committed the Washbridge robbery. They weren't caught on CCTV, and there are no witnesses. The other strange thing is that they took very little money. According to the bank manager, it was just about enough to fill a single bag. The two MOs bear no resemblance to one another. Hopefully, the powers-that-be will realise that, and treat them separately because the sooner I get shot of Riley the better. How was your evening?"

"Okay. I had a chat with Megan last night. I've invited her and her boyfriend over for dinner."

"Good. I'm glad you and she have buried the hatchet."

"There's no hatchet to bury."

"If you say so. Who's this boyfriend of hers?"

"I've no idea. I'm looking forward to meeting him, though."

***

I'd arranged to meet the NOCA committee at Chuckle House. Don Keigh and Ray Carter were seated, but Andrew Clowne was standing at the far end of the table. On the table in front of him was a black bag with a zip fastening.

"Are you absolutely sure about this, Jill?" Andrew Clowne said. "It seems an awfully dangerous mission for a woman to undertake."

"I'll be fine. This is what I do for a living." I picked up the bag. "Where is the drop off?"

Andrew Clowne took a sheet of paper from his pocket. "This note came this morning. You are to take the money to the bridge over the Wash—the one next to the hospital."

"Whereabouts on the bridge am I supposed to leave it?"

"There's a wastepaper bin in the centre of the bridge, on the right-hand side as you walk from the hospital. You're to wedge it behind the bin, and then leave the scene immediately."

"What time am I supposed to make the drop?"

"He's very specific about that. It must be left there at eleven thirty-eight on the dot. Not a minute earlier; not a minute later. Then you're to leave the scene immediately. He says he'll be watching, and if he sees anything he doesn't like, the deal is off."

"He's chosen a good location." I picked up the bag. "It would be practically impossible to keep an eye on the bag unless you're actually on the bridge. He could easily drive up in a car, stop just long enough to pick up the money, and be gone again in seconds."

"Who's to say he'll be in a car?" Ray Carter said. "He might have an accomplice who could pick up the bag, and throw it to a boat waiting under the bridge."

I checked my watch. It was a quarter to eleven. "I'd better get going or I might not make it in this traffic."

"Be careful, Jill," Don Keigh called after me.

"Yes, don't take any unnecessary risks," Ray Carter said.

***

I parked around the back of the hospital from where it was only a couple of minutes' walk to the bridge. If I had anything to do with it, this scumbag wasn't going to get away with the money. But it wasn't going to be easy to follow whoever collected the bag without being spotted.

It was the designated time, so I walked slowly to the centre of the bridge. When I reached the bin, I checked my watch again. It was eleven thirty- seven. I waited until the minute hand clicked over to eleven thirty-eight, and then wedged the bag behind the bin.

Mission accomplished, I hurried back off the bridge. I had no time to lose, so I dodged down the first alleyway I came to, cast the 'invisible' spell, and then ran back onto the bridge.

To my relief, the bag was still there. I'd deliberately laid it on its side, and unfastened the zip just a quarter of an inch. Still invisible, I cast the 'shrink' spell, and then climbed through the gap in the zip. It was dark inside; I couldn't see a thing.

I didn't have long to wait because, less than a minute later, someone picked up the bag, which sent me tumbling back and forth. Whoever had collected the bag was on foot, and obviously running. That was bad news for me—I was being thrown around in the dark interior.

Thankfully, that didn't last for long. The scumbag stopped, and placed the bag on its base. This was it. As soon as he opened the zip, I'd make my escape, reverse the two spells, and then make him sorry he'd ever been born.

The zip slid slowly open, and light shone into the bag. For the first time, I could see the contents—it wasn't what I'd expected.

Above me, looking down into the bag, was a man in his mid-thirties. He was unshaven and had unkempt hair.

But he was of no interest to me now.

I slipped out through the open zip. The bag was on the ground, next to a bench beside the river—no more than a few hundred yards from the bridge. I made my escape, found a quiet spot, and reversed both spells.

I now felt sure I knew who was behind the extortion threat. I just needed to work out why they had done it.

***

En route back to my car, I walked past the bank which Slippery Sam had robbed. Poor old Blaze. He was in for a whole heap of trouble once Daze got back from her holiday.

I could see how being able to transform into a snake would help the robber to get in and out of the bank, but that wouldn't help him to make a getaway with the money. To do that, he'd surely have to transform into a man again. So why hadn't he been caught on CCTV?

And then I noticed something. Something which might just save Blaze's bacon. I made a call.

"Blaze, it's Jill. Look, I've had an idea about Slippery Sam. It might prove to be nothing."

"Anything's better than what I have now."

"Have you seen which shop is in the building adjacent to the bank?"

"I can't say I've taken much notice."

"P For Pets."

"I still don't understand."

"According to Jack, the police found nothing on CCTV, and have no witnesses to the robber's getaway after the Washbridge bank robbery."

"That doesn't surprise me. They wouldn't have been looking for a snake."

"He may have got into the bank in snake form, but he wouldn't be able to make off with the money unless he changed back into a man. In which case, why didn't the CCTV pick him up?"

"I hadn't thought of that."

"What if he decided to lie low with the money, and wait until everything has settled down."

"What are you saying, Jill?"

"I'm saying that if that was his plan, then what better place for a snake to lie low than in a pet shop? Maybe he never actually came back outside, but found a way through to the shop next door? It's a big store. I'm sure there's lots of places in there where he could stash the money."

"It's worth a shot. I'll get over there straight away."

"Okay. Good luck."

***

My plate was pretty full what with murder, extortion, a timeshare scam and bank robberies. To say nothing of the witchfinder who had moved in across the road. But more worrying than all of those combined was the thought that it was Grandma's birthday in two days' time, and I still hadn't bought her a present.

It occurred to me that maybe if the twins and I put our heads together, between us we might come up with something, so I magicked myself over to Cuppy C. The twins' new assistants were working behind the counters. Amber and Pearl were seated at the window table, both eating muffins. It seemed rude not to join them in the muffinfest, so I ordered a latte and a blueberry muffin, and then went and sat with the girls.

"You two look busy."

"We've been run off our feet today, Jill," Amber said, tucking into a Black Forest muffin. "We can't all laze around like you do in the human world."

"Laze around?" I took a bite of my muffin. "I'll have you know I'm working on three cases, at the moment. And, I'm worried about Grandma's birthday; I haven't come up with a present for her yet. I thought if the three of us put our heads together we might be able to come up with a few good ideas. What do you think?"

"No need." Amber grinned. "I've already bought the perfect gift for Grandma."

"Not as good as the one I've got for her," Pearl said.

"Hold on. Do you mean to tell me that you two have already bought presents?"

They both nodded, and couldn't have looked any more smug if they'd tried.

"Come on then. Tell me what you've bought."

"I'm sorry," Amber said. She didn't look sorry. "But if I told you, I'd have to kill you."

"What about you, Pearl?"

"Sorry." She didn't look sorry either. "It's top secret."

They both giggled.

"Well, thanks for nothing, you two."

"You'll think of something," Amber said. "Maybe."

"Yeah." Pearl nodded. "No pressure."

"I'll remember this. Just wait until you two need my help." I stood up. "I'll go and talk to Aunt Lucy. I'm sure she'll be happy to give me some ideas."

"Good luck!" They called after me.

Aunt Lucy was cleaning the oven when I arrived. "Would you like a drink, Jill?"

"No, thanks. I can't stay long. I just wanted to pick your brain about Grandma's birthday present."

"What about it?"

"I wondered if we could kick around some ideas as to what we can buy for her?"

"I've already bought her a present."

"Oh? What did you get?"

She hesitated. "I'd rather not say."

"Why?"

"It took me ages to find just the right thing. And, well, I'm not being funny, but I don't want someone else to buy the same present. You do understand, don't you?"

"Oh yes, I understand. I understand that you and the twins have thrown me under the bus."

"That's a bit harsh, Jill. I'll gladly try to think of something for you to buy."

"It's okay. Don't trouble yourself. I'm sure I'll come up with something."

"Okay, dear, but if you get stuck, just give me a call."

"Is Barry upstairs?"

"No, Dolly popped in a few minutes ago. She's taken him for a walk with Babs. She'll be in the park if you want to try to catch them."

"I don't think I'll bother. I'll just check on Hamlet."

I was still grumbling to myself about the birthday present subterfuge, as I made my way upstairs. Hamlet was standing behind what looked like a mini easel. In his hands, he had a paintbrush and paint palette. At the opposite side of the cage a female hamster had grabbed a dressing gown to cover herself.

"Do you mind?" Hamlet looked and sounded annoyed. "You're disturbing an artist at work."

"I'm sorry. I had no idea that you were into painting."

"I'm not *'into painting,'* as you so eloquently put it; *I* am an artist."

"Sorry. That's what I meant."

"If you must know, I got the idea from that woman who sometimes takes Barry for a walk. Dolly, I think her name is. She brought a few of her paintings for me to see. My goodness! Have you seen her work?"

"I have, actually."

"Then you'll know what I'm talking about. After seeing those, I decided I couldn't do any worse. Gillian is here to model for me."

"Hi," Gillian said. She was obviously still embarrassed by my intrusion.

"Hi. I'm sorry to have barged in like this."

"Anyway," Hamlet said. "If you don't mind, we are rather busy."

"Of course. Bye then. Bye, Gillian. Nice to have met you."

Surreal.

Chapter 20

Wow! I might have expected such treachery from the twins, but I never would have thought that Aunt Lucy would abandon me too. Well, I'd show them. I'd find the best present ever for Grandma—one which would put their feeble offerings to shame.

Easier said than done, unfortunately. I'd spent the last hour walking around all the major shops in Washbridge, and so far, had not seen a single thing which I thought would fit the bill.

Exhausted, I dropped into a tiny tea room located on one of the back streets close to the bus station. It was called Tea Hee, and had a picture of a smiley face drinking a cup of tea as its logo.

I ordered a pot of tea for one, and eyed the display of muffins at the counter. I was conscious that I'd already had a blueberry muffin in Cuppy C. For that reason, I resisted the temptation to buy another, and instead bought a small strawberry cupcake.

What? It was only a small one! Sheesh!

As I ate the cupcake, I stared idly out of the window. And then I saw it. Immediately across the road from the tea room was a small specialist shop that would provide me with the ideal present for Grandma. Eat your heart out Aunt Lucy, Amber and Pearl.

The assistant in the shop had given me a strange look when I'd asked if she could gift-wrap my purchase. I couldn't think why.

I'd just put it into the boot of my car when my phone rang. It was the woman herself.

"Hello, Grandma."

"Get down to Ever!"

"You forgot the magic word."

"Now!"

"What's this all about?"

"I'll tell you when you get down here." And with that, she ended the call.

A woman of few words, that was Grandma. She could be infuriating, but I couldn't simply ignore her request in case she had more news about the witchfinder.

"Have you made it up with Megan, yet?" Kathy asked, as soon as I walked through the door of Ever.

"Yes, but no thanks to you. Where's Grandma?"

"Sunning herself." Kathy gestured towards the roof.

I made my way up the stairs, and onto the roof terrace where the temperature seemed even higher than the last time I'd been there. Once again, the terrace garden was full of people sunning themselves, and knitting.

It took me a few moments, but then I spotted Grandma lying on a sun lounger at the far side of the roof terrace. She was wearing shorts and a vest top. Let me tell you, it was not a pretty sight.

"You called, Grandma?"

She sat up, removed her sunglasses, and took a sip of her cocktail.

"This is rather good," she commented. "You really should try one."

"I can't drink. I have to drive home. What did you want me for?"

"Sit down." She pointed to the vacant deckchair next to her.

Deckchairs and I had a history. I was hopeless at

putting them up, and nervous of sitting in them.

"It's okay. I prefer to stand."

"As you wish." She reached underneath the sun lounger, and pulled out a small, white cardboard box. "There you go." She handed it to me.

"What is it?"

"Open it, and take a look."

I nervously pulled open the lid. Inside were six miniature syringes each of them filled with a blue liquid.

"What's this?"

"Shush! We don't want anyone else to see them. It's Brewflower."

"Where did you get it?"

"Never mind that. Just make sure that you've got one of the syringes with you at all times. If the witchfinder strikes, and he will, plunge one into him. But don't hesitate or it'll be too late."

"Okay, thanks." I closed the lid, and slid the box into my bag.

When I made to leave, Grandma grabbed my hand. "I trust that you've picked out a nice present for my birthday?"

"I have. I think you'll really like it."

***

It seemed obvious to me that the owner of the Merry Widows forum must be behind the timeshare scam. No one else had access to the postal addresses of the members. To my surprise and delight, I discovered that the owner of the forum hadn't bothered to hide his details when registering the domain name. The owner was a J.E.

Penn who lived in New Manston, which was a fifteen-minute drive from Washbridge. The semi-detached house was unremarkable in a street full of identical houses.

"Yes?" A spotty young man, wearing jogging bottoms and a baggy sweatshirt answered the door.

"Are you J.E. Penn?"

"Yeah. Jonathan."

Now I was confused. Mrs Rollo, Lily Padd and Kathy had all described the timeshare conman as being in his late fifties or early sixties, and bald.

"Are you the owner of the Merry Widows forum?"

"Yeah, but I'm not responsible for what people post on there, so if someone has upset you, don't blame me."

"This is much more important than that. Can I come in and talk to you?"

"No."

"Okay. If you'd rather I call the police, then you can answer their questions instead."

"There's no need to involve the police." He hesitated. "I suppose you'd better come in."

He led the way into what had probably once been a dining room, but which now looked more like a student's bedsit. On the table, was a computer and at least five empty pizza boxes.

"What's this all about?" He sounded nervous.

"A number of your members have been conned out of significant amounts of money."

"That's got nothing to do with me."

"Whoever did it found their victims on your forum. And, unless I'm mistaken you're the only person who has access to the postal addresses of your members."

"That's true, but I'm not a conman. I work at the local

bingo hall — behind the bar. The forum is just a side-line, which earns me a few extra quid from advertising. That's all."

"Do you live here alone?"

"No. This is my parents' house. They're both out at work."

I glanced around, and caught sight of a photograph on the sideboard.

"Who's that?"

"My mum and dad."

"How long ago was it taken?"

"I don't know. Twenty years probably."

"And does your dad still look like that?"

"He wishes. He's bald now."

"What does he do for a living?"

"He's a butcher."

Penn Butchers was only three streets away, so I left the car, and made my way there on foot. There were no customers in the shop, so once I was inside, I turned the sign over so it read 'Closed'.

"What do you think you're doing?" the bald-headed man behind the counter said.

"Mr Penn, I take it?"

"Who are you? Turn that sign around!"

"Not until we've had a chance to talk."

"About what?"

"Oh, I don't know. Holidays, maybe? What about timeshare holidays? I might be interested in a good timeshare deal. Do you know of any?"

His expression changed, and he grabbed the meat cleaver on the bench in front of him. "Get out! I have nothing to say to you."

"That's a pity because I have a lot to say to you. I take it that your son, Jonathan, isn't aware that you've been trawling his forum for targets for your sordid little timeshare scam?"

"Get out!" He was red in the face now. "Get out or you'll be sorry."

I cast the 'illusion' spell.

"Am I supposed to be afraid of a lollipop?"

He glanced at the cleaver, but instead saw a large round lollipop. Confused, he threw it onto the floor. The next thing I knew, he'd leapt over the counter, and was headed for the door.

I combined an enchantment spell with the 'tie-up' spell, to bind him hand and foot with several links of sausage. When he tried to protest, I stuffed a black pudding into his mouth. That would keep him quiet for a while.

I jumped over the counter, opened the till, and took out the day's takings. After pocketing those, I scribbled a note giving full details of the timeshare scam perpetrated by the butcher, and left it on the counter. On my way out, I made an anonymous call, using a 'burner' phone, to the local police, and told them they would find the man responsible for several timeshare scams tied up in Penn Butchers.

***

It was late when I got back to Washbridge, but I decided to call into the office just in case there were any urgent messages waiting for me. Mrs V had already gone home, but she'd left a note on her desk which read: *there are no messages.*

It had been a long day, but overall I felt that it had been a most productive one. I'd caught the timeshare conman, and was now sure I knew who was behind the NOCA extortion demands.

I was just about to leave when I caught a whiff of something. Something fishy. And it was coming from my office.

"Do you mind?" Winky was dressed in an evening suit, and looked quite dapper. Sitting at the table with him was a female cat in a pretty red dress.

"Sorry. I didn't realise you were entertaining."

"I did tell you." Winky sighed. "Peggy, this is Jill. My human."

"Pleased to meet you, Peggy. How's the food?"

"Excellent," Winky said.

"What's going on here?" The voice came from the windowsill. It was Bella, and she didn't look a happy pussy.

"Bella?" Winky looked horrified.

"Who's that?" Peggy said.

"'*That*' is Winky's girlfriend." Bella spat the words.

"Girlfriend?" Peggy glared at Winky. "You told me you weren't in a relationship."

"You told her what?" Bella screamed.

Winky looked like a pussy caught in the headlights. "There's a simple explanation for all of this." He glanced from one of the cats to the other.

"Save it!" Peggy stood up, and slapped him across the face. Then both she and Bella disappeared out of the window.

Winky sat down; he looked shell-shocked.

"Shame to let all this food go to waste," I said, taking a seat at the table.

What? Who are you calling heartless? I was hungry.

***

Back in Smallwash, I paid a visit to Mrs Rollo.

"Jill? I'm glad you came over, I was going to come around to see you."

"Oh? What about?"

"I don't like to speak out of turn, but I'm a little worried about the new man across the road."

"Worried why?"

"Earlier today, there was the strangest noise coming from his house."

"What kind of noise?"

"I don't really know how to describe it. A kind of high-pitched wailing sound, as though a small creature was being tortured. Normally, I would have gone over and said something, but to be honest, he gives me the creeps."

"He is a little strange, isn't he? Thanks for the tip-off." I took out the money I'd taken from the butcher's till. "This is for you."

"I don't understand?"

"It's a small part of the money that was taken from you by the conman. He's been arrested, and should be charged with a number of similar scams. You may get your money back in time, but unfortunately, I can't guarantee that. At least this will go some way towards compensating you."

"I can't take your money, Jill."

"This isn't my money. It belonged to the conman. He insisted that you have it."

Chapter 21

Overnight, I'd been thinking about what Mrs Rollo had said. Rory Kilbride was up to something, and whatever it was, it had me worried. I couldn't just stand around and wait for him to make a move. It was time for me to take the initiative—to strike first. But I would need help from someone who could keep a watch on the witchfinder without drawing too much attention to themselves. And who better than Rory Kilbride's next door neighbour?

I waited until after Jack had gone to work, and then a little longer until Jen had left the house. As soon as she'd gone, I went over to Blake's.

"Jill? You're an early bird."

"Can I come in?"

He led the way through to the kitchen.

"Do you want a drink?"

"No. I'm not staying. I'm here to ask for your help."

"Anything. You've helped me often enough."

"It's your neighbour. The witchfinder."

"You're certain it's him, then?"

"Ninety-nine per cent, but I haven't been able to get a look at the nape of his neck yet. Once I'm sure he has the goblet tattoo, I'll be able to act. But I need your help."

"You want me to look for the tattoo?"

"No. That would be much too dangerous, but if I'm going to tackle him, I need to know more about the man."

"What kind of thing?"

"Anything that you think might be useful. Does he ever have any visitors? Does he go out and come back at the same time each day? Also, if you would listen for any unusual noises, that could be useful. Mrs Rollo told me she heard some strange sounds coming from his house."

"What kind of sounds?"

"She didn't know, but it had her freaked out. The more you can tell me about the man, the better placed I'll be when the time comes to make my move. I need you to be my eyes and ears when I'm not around."

"Of course. I'll do what I can, but I still don't like the idea of you acting alone."

"I'll be okay. Better to strike first than to wait for him to make a move."

***

My phone rang. It was Blaze.

"You were right, Jill! Thank you so much."

"He was in the pet shop?"

"Yeah. He took a bit of finding because they have an awful lot of real snakes in there. I brought in a couple more rogue retrievers, and between us we managed to flush him out. He's back behind bars in Candlefield now."

"That's great. What about the money?"

"It's still inside the bank."

"How do you mean?"

"Once we'd arrested him, he agreed to give up the location of the cash. It wasn't going to do him any good back in Candlefield, and I persuaded him that it might mean a lighter sentence."

"So, where is it?"

"Slippery Sam had found a way to get in and out of the bank from the pet shop, but he could only do it while in snake form. He hid the money in the bank with the intention of going back to collect it once all the fuss had died down. It's in a bag underneath one of the large artificial plants—there's plenty of room in those giant pots. The plants normally get swapped out about once every six months. Guess who was going to turn up, posing as an operative from the company that supplies the plants?"

"Slippery Sam."

"Precisely. He'd already organised the van and uniform."

"Is the money still there? Underneath the plant?"

"Yeah, but not for long. I've posted a note through the letterbox, addressed to the bank manager, telling him where he'll find his money."

"I wonder what he'll make of that?"

"I'd like to be a fly on the wall when he looks under the plant. Anyway, thanks again, Jill. You may have saved my job."

"No problem, Blaze. Glad I could help."

***

I was confident that I knew who was behind the NOCA extortion demands, but I didn't want to show my hand until I had covered all the bases. Mr Bobo, the clown who'd just been murdered, had lived not far from Washbridge. It had taken me a while to contact his widow who was no doubt trying to avoid the press. When I finally managed to get hold of her, and explained that I was working for NOCA, she agreed to see me.

The quaint little bungalow was called 'The Little Top'. Barbara Berry was in her mid-sixties.

"Thank you for seeing me, Mrs Berry."

"Anything to help bring Bobo's murderer to justice."

She must have seen the puzzled look on my face because she continued, "It must sound strange to hear me call him Bobo, but it's what I used to call him all the time. His name was Percival, but he hated that, and he hated Percy even more. Did you know that we were a double act?"

"No, I had no idea."

"I went under the name of Lulu. Bobo and Lulu."

"Was that what he called you? Lulu?"

"No." She managed a weak smile. "Only on stage. I was always Barb to him."

The living room was full of photographs—most of them of Bobo and Lulu.

"I was the one who got him into clowning," she said. "I've been obsessed with them since I was a child."

"It appears that you both enjoyed it."

"We did. After the kids had grown up and left home, it became our life. We only ever did it for charitable events; we never made any money out of it. But we had a lot of fun, and we gave a lot of pleasure to others."

"I take it that the police are treating this as murder?"

"At the moment, they're calling it a suspicious death, but I don't see that it can be anything other than murder."

"I realise this is difficult for you, but do you think you could talk me through exactly what happened?"

"I'll do my best." She took a seat in one of the armchairs. I sat opposite her, on the sofa. "Bobo was trying out a new prop—an exploding dicky bow. It should just have made a loud bang, and given off a lot of smoke. But instead, it practically took his head off."

She began to cry. I waited several minutes until she was

able to compose herself again.

"Did he by any chance buy the prop from Clown's List?"

"No. It just appeared on the doorstep."

"Didn't you think that was rather suspicious?"

"Not really. It was wrapped as a birthday present. It had been Bobo's birthday two weeks earlier, and we just assumed someone had forgotten. He often received props like this as presents from his friends in the clown community."

"Do you have the wrapping paper or box that it came in?"

"No. The police asked the same thing, but I put it in the bin, and it was taken away by the garbage men on the same day that Bobo died. I asked the police if they'd be able to find it, but they said it would be like looking for a needle in a haystack."

We talked for just under an hour. Most of that time was taken up with Barbara reminiscing about her late husband, and the happy times they'd shared as Bobo and Lulu.

***

I'd heard enough. Now it was time for me to act on my suspicions. For this particular phone call, I was going to use one of my many 'burner' phones because I didn't want the person I was calling to recognise my number.

It was time for all my acting prowess to once again come into play.

"Is that Andrew Clowne?" Not even my own sister would have recognised the voice I used.

"Speaking?"

"Andrew, thank goodness I was able to contact you. My name is Patricia Delmore. I'm associate producer at Clown TV. One of the articles we were due to run today has fallen through at the last minute, so I have a spot that I need to fill quickly. I understand that it's your final year as chairman of NOCA?"

"That's right, Patricia."

"I thought it might make an interesting article to cover the period of your chairmanship. All the things you've achieved etc, etc."

"I can see how that would be interesting to your viewers."

"The thing is, Andrew, I would need you to get up here straightaway."

"Where?"

"To our studio in Birmingham."

"That would take me at least two hours."

"If it's too far, I understand."

"No, not at all. I'll get straight in the car now."

"Excellent. I look forward to seeing you shortly."

I gave it thirty minutes, and then phoned Don Keigh and Ray Carter, using my regular phone. I asked both men to meet me at Chuckle House immediately on an important matter relating to the upcoming conference.

"Andrew has been called away," Don Keigh said when he arrived. "Something about a TV programme."

"It doesn't matter." I waved away his concern. "I'm sure the two of you will be able to sort this out. Basically, I've received information which has left me concerned about the upcoming conference."

"What kind of information?" Ray Carter said.

"There really isn't time to go into the details. You're just going to have to trust me on this one. If you can give me access to NOCA records, including access to the computer, then I'm sure I'll be able to get this resolved very quickly. Certainly, in time for the conference."

"I'm not sure." Don Keigh hesitated. "Andrew usually deals with all that kind of stuff."

"But Andrew isn't here, and I'm sure that he'd want this issue resolved, so as not to jeopardise the conference. Don't you think?"

The two men looked at one another, but then Ray Carter nodded. "Of course — anything you need. Come this way."

They led me to a much smaller office just along the corridor. Don Keigh unlocked the door, and showed me inside.

"We really don't have all that much paperwork — just these two filing cabinets. Everything else is on there." He pointed to the desktop computer which looked like it had seen better days.

"What about the login information?"

"Andrew keeps it in the top drawer," Ray Carter said. "I know that's not the way things should be done, but no one ever comes in here."

I pulled out the drawer, and took out the notebook, which had the user ID and password written on the inside cover. Moments later, I was in.

"Thanks for that, gentlemen. You can leave this with me now."

"Maybe we should stay with you?" Don Keigh said.

I'd been worried they might suggest that, so I quickly

cast the 'forget' spell on both of them, and then led them to the outer door.

"Thanks, gentlemen. That's been a great help."

Both men looked a little confused, but bid me farewell, and went on their way. Once I was sure they'd gone, I went back inside, and began my search through NOCA records.

Two hours later, I had everything I needed.

***

Jack was in a good mood because the combined Washbridge/West Chipping operation was over.

"The money was inside the bank all along," he said.

"Where?"

"Under a pot plant, if you can believe it."

"Why would the robbers have left it there?"

"We assume they intended coming back for it later, but who knows? Nothing about this makes any sense. We still have no sign of the robber or robbers on CCTV."

"How did you find the money?"

"We didn't. The bank manager did. Someone left him a note."

"Who?"

"No idea. It was signed: 'Blaze'."

"Do you think that 'Blaze' was the robber?"

"I've no idea, and frankly, I don't care. I'm just glad I won't have to work with that idiot, Riley, any longer." Jack glanced out of the front window. "Megan and her boyfriend are on their way around."

Normally, I hated entertaining, but I was pleased to have the chance to redeem myself with Megan.

"I'll get it." I made for the door.

Megan looked terrific. She was wearing a simple blue knee-length dress and low heels. But then, she looked good in everything she wore.

"Jill, this is Harry."

The young man standing next to her was tall, dark and handsome. His teeth almost blinded me when he flashed a smile.

"Come in both of you. Jack's in the lounge. Harry, why don't you go through and introduce yourself. I'd like a quick word with Megan."

When I was sure that Harry was out of earshot, I whispered to her, "Please don't say anything about the paint incident to Jack, will you?"

"No, of course not. I know now that it wasn't your fault."

"Thanks. I really appreciate that."

Although I say it myself, dinner wasn't at all bad. And no, I hadn't brought in outside caterers. It was all my own work.

I couldn't help but like Megan. In some ways, she was ridiculously naive, but she was good-natured and obviously very genuine. That was more than I could say for her boyfriend. Harry was full of himself, and so very vain. I caught him checking his reflection in the mirror numerous times during the evening. He had only one topic of conversation: himself. And yet, whenever I tried to find out what he did for a living, he changed the subject.

***

"Thank goodness that's over," I said, after we'd seen them out.

"I thought it went pretty well." Jack was clearing away the dishes. "I don't know what she sees in him, though. Did you see him keep checking the mirror?"

"Yeah. And he's so boring. Why do you think he was so secretive about his job?"

"Maybe he's a spy?" Jack laughed.

"She could do much better. Still, Kathy will be pleased to know that Megan's got herself a boyfriend."

"I have to say, Jill, you really surpassed yourself with the meal tonight—it was delicious."

"It's nice of you to say so, kind sir. And I know just how you can show your gratitude."

He grinned, took my hand, and began to lead me to the stairs.

"Actually, I meant you could do the washing up."

Chapter 22

"Are you alright, Jill?" Jack asked. We were at the kitchen table, eating breakfast. "You've barely said a word since we got up."

"I'm fine. I was just thinking about a couple of cases I'm working on."

I couldn't tell Jack the truth, which was that I was feeling as nervous as a kitten because today was the day that I had to give a talk at CASS. Whatever had possessed me to agree to do it? As if speaking in public wasn't terrifying enough, I was about to visit a place where dragons and other scary creatures roamed freely. And to top it all, I had to travel there by airship. I didn't like travelling on aeroplanes, so how was I meant to cope with being on an airship?

I barely touched my breakfast; I just didn't have the stomach for it. To avoid any more awkward questions from Jack, I made an excuse about an early meeting, and set off on my way. The sooner I got this over with the better.

***

The departure point for the airship to CASS was located close to the Black Mountains. I magicked myself over there well ahead of time. There was a turnstile just inside the door. Behind it, was seated a man wearing a green uniform and peaked cap. The words: 'CASS Airship' were printed on both his blazer pocket, and his cap.

"Ticket please." He held out his hand.

I dug into my bag, and pulled out the two tickets which

had been posted to me. I found the one for the outward journey, and handed it to him. He studied it for a moment, then stamped it, and handed it back.

"The waiting room is down there on the left. The toilets are on the right. There are no toilets on the airship, so I would suggest that you pay a visit before departure."

"How long is the journey?"

"Usually about forty minutes—depending on weather conditions."

I did as he suggested and went to the loo. When I walked through to the waiting room, I was surprised to find a man sitting on one of the benches. He looked equally surprised to see me.

"Good morning." His smile filled his round face. The man was almost as broad as he was tall. His unruly hair was a mix of black and grey.

"Morning. You're going to CASS too, I take it?"

"I'd better be. It's the only stop the airship makes." He laughed. "Are you going to see about the kitchen job?"

"No, I'm actually going to give a talk."

"He stood up, walked over to me, and offered his hand. "You must be Jill Gooder. Sorry, I should have realised. I've seen the posters about your talk."

"There are posters?"

"Oh, yes. There's been a lot of excitement among the pupils. It isn't every day they're visited by a level seven witch."

"I'm not actually level seven."

"I realise you declined the offer, but still, you're quite the celebrity."

Oh bum!

"A number of kitchen staff have left recently. One under

rather unfortunate circumstances. I'm sorry I confused you for one of the new applicants."

"No problem. You said 'unfortunate circumstances'?"

"There are strict rules for venturing outside the walls of CASS. Bertie Baxter thought he knew better and disregarded them. Terrible business. Have you ever seen a destroyer dragon?"

"I have, actually. In the Levels Competition."

"Then you'll know they're not to be trifled with, as Bertie found out to his cost. I should introduce myself. I'm Reginald Crowe, but everyone calls me Reggie. I'm the caretaker and general handyman at CASS. I was given compassionate leave to visit my mother who's been ill."

"I'm sorry to hear that."

"She's much better now. Made of tough stuff, my mum."

"I'm feeling really rather nervous about today," I admitted.

"I don't blame you. Public speaking terrifies me."

"I'm a little nervous about the speech, but I'm much more nervous about travelling on the airship, if I'm honest."

"I shouldn't worry about that. It's actually quite a pleasant experience. I love the journey, particularly when, like today, there are only a few people travelling. It's a different kettle of fish at the start and end of term when it's full of pupils. They can get a little rowdy, as you can imagine."

"I'm not very comfortable with air travel at the best of times. I'm always nervous on aeroplanes. Isn't it rather a bumpy ride on the airship?"

"Most of the time it's fine, but occasionally there is

turbulence. And, of course, if there's a thunderstorm, things can get a little hairy. But the weather looks fine today, so you shouldn't have anything to worry about."

"What about the dragons? Do they ever attack the airship?"

"It travels way too high for them. The only time there can be a problem is when it descends to land. Occasionally a dragon might take a look to see if there's anything to eat."

"I don't like the sound of that."

"The airship is fitted with defences which can keep the dragons at bay. You really have nothing to worry about."

"Have you worked at CASS long, Reggie?"

"Man and boy. My father was the caretaker before me; I followed in his footsteps. I couldn't be happier."

"What sort of reception do you think I'll get from the pupils?"

"The majority will be keen to hear what you have to say about the human world. There'll probably be a few rowdy ones, as there are at any school. They may try to give you a hard time, but it'll be nothing you can't handle, I'm sure."

Just then an announcement came over the Tannoy.

"The airship will be docking in two minutes. Two minutes until the airship docks. All passengers please prepare to board."

A set of double doors to my right slid open. Beyond them was a short walkway similar to those used to board an aeroplane. Through the windows on either side of the walkway, I could now see the airship, which was anchored to the ground at the side of the building.

"It's a lot smaller than I was expecting," I said, as

Reggie and I started down the short walkway.

"This is one of the mini airships. They use much larger ones at the beginning and end of term, but it makes sense to use these smaller ones for one-off trips like this."

Reggie pressed the orange button to open the door onto the airship. Once on board the gondola, we had to climb a staircase up to the small oval lounge. There were padded benches along the walls, and others which ran the width of the lounge. Reggie beckoned me to join him on the bench which looked out over the front of the airship.

"Where's the driver?" I asked.

"Driver?" He laughed. "I think you mean the pilot. He's below us. The cockpit is underneath here."

I felt the airship jerk slightly to one side, and instinctively, I grabbed the handrail.

"It's okay," Reggie reassured me. "They've released the anchors. Look! We're starting to rise."

I looked out of the window, and could see that we were slowly lifting off the ground. The butterflies in my stomach were going crazy, but there was no turning back now. Fortunately, the ascent was slow and very smooth. I'd been worried that I might feel sick, but I was fine.

The ascent continued until the buildings below appeared to be little more than a model village. After no more than ten minutes, the landscape below had changed completely. Gone were all the buildings; we were now journeying over vast areas of wasteland, forests and mountain ranges.

"I had no idea the paranormal world covered such a large area," I said.

"Most sups only ever see the highly-populated regions, but in fact that's only a very small portion of the paranormal world. Of course, most of this region is uninhabitable."

All my fears about the airship journey had now evaporated, and I was able to enjoy the scenery below.

"Have you met Desdemona Nightowl, yet?" Reggie asked.

"Yes, she came to visit me at my house, to see whether or not I intended to give the talk."

"She's a very formidable woman, as I'm sure you'll discover. She's only been in the post a few years, but she's already made her mark."

"I understand that the building used to belong to the Wrongacre family many years ago?"

"That's right. Charles Wrongacre left the building and grounds to the Combined Sup Council to do with as they saw fit. They were the ones who decided to create CASS. It was a brave and very surprising decision, but it seems to have paid off. There are still lots of Wrongacre family heirlooms to be seen around the building. In fact, very little has changed since the Wrongacre days. If you get the chance to explore it, I'm sure you'll find it fascinating."

A few minutes later, I could sense that the airship was beginning its descent. I checked the windows on all sides in case there were any dragons nearby. Thankfully, there were none to be seen.

"Look!" Reggie pointed. "That's CASS over there."

The building, which had four tall towers, was much bigger than I'd expected, and the grounds much more extensive. A high wall circled the estate.

"It's a very impressive building." I had my nose pressed to the glass.

"And huge. I've lived there more or less all of my life,

and I still haven't managed to explore all of it."

"Where does the airship land?"

"On the playing fields at the rear of the building."

I braced myself, but I needn't have worried because the landing was so smooth that I hadn't even realised we were on the ground.

We had to wait a few minutes until the airship had been anchored. While we did, I spotted a strange little open-topped vehicle speeding across the playing fields towards us. It looked like some kind of hovercraft, which appeared to be steering itself. There were only five people in the vehicle—a man and four pupils: two girls and two boys.

Eventually, the airship's door slid open, and I followed Reggie down the steps.

"You must be Jill," the man had now alighted from the hovercraft. "I'm Cuthbert Bluegrass—the deputy head. Ms Nightowl apologises that she was unable to be here to greet you, but something—err—important has come up."

"No problem. Nice to meet you."

"I need to have a word with Reggie," he said, already walking away. "But if you'd like to climb aboard the 'hoverette', these pupils will give you a quick tour. Then you can meet up with myself and the headmistress a little later."

"Sure. That's fine."

I climbed aboard the hoverette. "Morning, guys."

The pupils nodded, but seemed more pre-occupied with what the deputy head was doing. He was now in conversation with Reggie who, if I wasn't mistaken, looked more than a little concerned about something.

Without warning, the hoverette sprang into life. After a

quick one hundred and eighty degree turn, it began to speed towards the house.

"Who's driving this thing?" I asked.

"No driver required," one of the boys said. "It's all controlled by magic."

We were approaching the wall of the building at an alarming speed, and the hoverette showed no signs of slowing down. What an irony if I'd survived the airship journey only to be killed in a horrific crash in some silly little hovercraft.

"The wall!" I yelled, but none of the pupils seemed to be at all concerned.

We were only a matter of feet away from it, so I closed my eyes and waited for the impact, but there was none. A section of the wall had slid up to allow us to enter the building. We were now speeding along inside a clear plastic tube. Moments later, we came to a sudden halt, and my stomach lurched.

The pupils climbed out of the hoverette, and I followed them. We were standing on a platform—a kind of miniature version of a London underground station. The name plaque on the wall read 'North Tower'.

As soon as I'd disembarked, the hoverette shot off along the tube.

Chapter 23

"Wow!" I glanced around the platform. "I really hadn't expected anything like this."

"The hoverettes have been around for a while," one of the boys said. "But the underground tube system was only added quite recently. It's the quickest way to get around, but we're not normally allowed to use it. It's for the staff to get from one side of the building to the other. And, of course, for visitors such as yourself, Ms Gooder."

"Please, you must all call me Jill."

They looked a little unsure.

"The headmistress said that we should call you Ms Gooder," one of the girls said.

"I won't tell if you don't." I hoped my smile might reassure them. "And, it's about time I got to know your names."

"I'm Wendy Makeright," the young witch with the dark brown hair said. "I'm in Wrongacre house." She pointed to her tie, which had green and black stripes.

"I'm Jerome Wurlitzer," the young wizard standing next to her said. "I'm in Nomad house." He was wearing a red and black striped tie.

"I'm Terry Crabday." The other young wizard's tie had blue and black stripes. "I'm in Longstaff house."

"And I'm Sissy," the second young witch said. "Sissy Pontoon. I'm in Capstan house." Her tie had yellow and black stripes.

"Is something going on that I should know about?" I asked. "Everyone seems rather nervous. Including the four of you."

They exchanged glances, and I could sense that they

were unsure how to respond.

"Please, if there's something wrong, I'd rather know."

"We were told not to say anything." Jerome Wurlitzer pulled at the cuff of his blazer. "And besides, we're not really sure what has happened."

"Tell me what you do know, please."

"About thirty minutes before your airship arrived, the alarm went off."

"A fire alarm?"

"No, that's a different kind of alarm altogether. This is the 'general emergency' alarm. I've only ever heard it sound once before, and that was just a practice drill. Originally, we were meant to meet you in the headmistress's office later this morning, but then we got a message to say that we had to join the deputy head, and that we were to show you around the north tower. That's all we know, honestly."

"Okay. No problem. I guess we'll just carry on until we hear from the headmistress. How do you all like it at CASS?"

"I love it here," Sissy said.

"Me too."

"And me."

"Yeah, it's fantastic."

"And which is the best house?"

"Wrongacre, of course."

"Rubbish. Nomad is by far the best."

"In your dreams. Longstaff puts the others to shame."

"Obviously, it's Capstan."

They all seemed a little more relaxed now.

"We're supposed to take you up to the third floor," Wendy Makeright said. "That's where they teach the history of magic."

"To be honest, I'd rather see the Dragon Club."

"How do you know about that?" Terry Crabday looked surprised, as did the others.

"I've spoken to someone who attended CASS. She used to be a member of the Dragon Club. She's a rogue retriever now."

"I want to be a rogue retriever," Jerome Wurlitzer said. "I've even picked the name I'll use: Jaze."

"With a name like that, you should fit right in."

"We can't take you to see the Dragon Club," Sissy said. "It's held in the basement, and the doors are locked during the daytime. Only the headmistress and the head of dragon studies has a key. We could show you the library though. That's in the north tower, and it's pretty spectacular."

"Okay, why not? Lead the way."

I followed the kids up a narrow, winding staircase.

"No one is allowed to speak in the library." Terry Crabday hesitated as he turned the door handle.

"Sure. No problem."

Huge bookcases stretched from floor to high ceiling.

"How do you reach those up there?" I pointed to the books on the top shelves of the ludicrously tall bookcases.

"Shush!" Someone called out.

"Sorry."

"Shush!"

The woman, seated at the desk at the far side of the room, stood up, and walked over to us. The kids looked terrified, and when she got closer, I could see why. She made Grandma look attractive. The woman beckoned me to follow her, and led the way to a door located between two of the huge bookcases.

"I'm sorry about that," she said, once we were inside the small office. "My name is Natasha Fastjersey. I'm the head librarian. No talking is allowed in the library."

"I'm very sorry."

"You're Jill Gooder, aren't you?"

"That's right."

"I knew you were visiting today, but the headmistress hadn't warned me that you would be dropping into the library."

"It wasn't planned. The headmistress seems to have some kind of emergency on her hands."

"Yes, I heard the alarm."

"What's going on?"

"I don't know. I doubt it's anything too serious, or we would have heard by now."

"Is it okay if I look around the library?"

"Of course, but I must remind you again that there is strictly no talking."

"Understood."

I spent the best part of an hour exploring the library. Every book appeared to be a leather bound first edition. Huge ladders were located at the far end of each bookcase—these could be slid back and forth to provide access to the books on the higher shelves. I ventured half way up one, but went no further—I never did have a head for heights.

High on the wall, in between two of the bookcases, hung two large paintings—portraits of a man and a woman. It was obvious that at one time a third painting must have hung there, but now there was only an empty picture hook.

When it was time to leave, I waited until we were out of the library, and then asked about the paintings.

"The man is Charles Wrongacre," Sissy said. "The woman is his wife, Agnes Wrongacre—she died in childbirth."

"What used to be on the empty picture hook?"

"A portrait of Charles Wrongacre's only child, a son, once hung there. After his son died, Charles couldn't bear to see the painting—it broke his heart to do so. He had it taken down, and put into storage. When CASS took over the building, a search was made for the painting, so it could be rehung, but it was never found."

"Does anyone know how his son died?"

"Not as far as I know. It's something of a mystery. I've only ever heard it described as 'tragic circumstances'—whatever that means."

"Where would you like to go next, Jill?" Jerome Wurlitzer asked.

"I'd quite like to see your dorms, if that's possible."

The four kids looked at one another. My request had obviously taken them by surprise.

"I don't see why not," Wendy said, eventually. "They're in this block."

"Lead the way, then."

The dorms were not what I'd expected. The kids shared—two to a room.

"These are nice," I commented.

"It all depends who you're sharing with." Terry Crabday pulled a face. "I have to share with Scabby Davies."

"Have any of you seen dragons flying overhead?"

"It rarely happens, "Jerome said. "All the walls have

audio defences which are triggered automatically when a dragon approaches. The noises are designed to scare them away, and they do a pretty good job. I haven't seen a single dragon overhead all the time I've been here."

"I've seen one," Terry said.

"No, you haven't." Sissy scoffed.

"I have. Just before the end of last term."

"How come no one else reported it?"

Terry shrugged.

"You must have dreamt it," Wendy said.

"I did not dream it."

"Okay, guys!" I intervened. "Let's not fall out."

Just then, a voice came through the many speakers mounted along the corridors.

"Will Jill Gooder, and the pupils accompanying her, please make their way to my office immediately."

The voice was unmistakably that of Desdemona Nightowl.

The four kids looked panic stricken.

"She'll kill us," Wendy said. "We weren't meant to bring you in here."

"Don't worry. I'll tell the headmistress that I insisted. Come on, we don't want to keep her waiting."

Jerome led the way up to the top floor of the north tower. Sissy knocked on the double doors.

"Come in!" The headmistress was obviously annoyed. "Where have you children been? I told you to accompany Ms Gooder to the history of magic classroom."

The four kids looked terrified.

"It's my fault, headmistress. I asked them to show me the library and their dormitories. I hope you don't mind?"

"I suppose not." She took a deep breath. "You've

probably already realised that we have an 'incident' on our hands."

"The librarian mentioned something about an alarm?"

She turned to the kids. "Children, off you go. Straight back to your rooms and stay there."

"Thanks for showing me around," I called after them.

They'd no sooner left than an alarm sounded; it was deafening, but thankfully only lasted a few seconds.

"What's going on, Headmistress?"

"I'm really sorry about this, Ms Gooder. It couldn't have happened at a worse time."

"What do the alarms mean?"

"Shortly before you were due to arrive, the first alarm sounded because there had been a breach of the outer wall. That's why I couldn't be there to meet you."

"A breach? What does that mean?"

"We've been trying to establish exactly what happened. Occasionally a creature will damage the wall without actually getting into the grounds. We were hoping that was the case today."

"But it wasn't?"

"It seems not. The second alarm means that a creature has been seen inside the grounds."

"What kind of creature? A dragon?"

Before she could answer, two wizards, dressed in overalls, came rushing into the room. The look on both of their faces was the same—terror.

"What's happened?" the headmistress demanded.

"It's a pouchfeeder," the first wizard said. "It's got one of the boys."

The colour drained from the headmistress's face, and I had to grab her arm before she fell. "Who is it?" Her voice was weak now.

"Tommy Bestwick."

"We have to get down there, and stop the creature before it gets back out through the wall."

"We'll never make it," the second wizard said. "The wall was breached near the East Tower. The creature will be long gone before we can get there."

"Can't we just magic ourselves there?" I suggested.

"All magical powers are suppressed within the walls of CASS to stop the children misusing them. The only place you can use magic is in the magic labs, but they are at the other end of the school."

"Will the boy still be alive?" I asked.

"Yes, but only until the pouchfeeder gets him back to its nest. What will I tell his parents?"

"There's still time to save him!" I rushed out of the door, and back down the corridor that I'd walked along with the kids. When I reached the stairs, I took a left and followed another corridor to the end. Just as I'd expected, there was the suit of armour.

"What are you doing, Miss Gooder?" The headmistress and the wizards were coming up behind me.

"No time to explain. Just follow me." I grabbed the knight's axe, and then pressed his shield in the centre. As I did, the wall behind it slid open, and I stepped inside. After a few steps, the ground disappeared from under my feet, and I began to slide down a steep chute. I could hear voices behind me. The headmistress and the wizards were still following.

After no more than a few seconds, I saw a wall looming ahead of me. When I was only feet away, it slid upwards, and I shot through the gap. A little winded, I picked myself up off the grass. In front of me, no more than a hundred yards away, was the damaged section of the wall. I picked up the axe, which had fallen from my hand when I'd tumbled out of the chute, and ran towards the wall. Unless I was already too late, this would be where the creature was headed.

Moments later, the pouchfeeder appeared; it looked like a giant Tasmanian devil. The creature was coming towards me at a rate of knots. Out of the corner of my eye, I could see the headmistress and the two wizards heading my way too, but the creature would be upon me long before they covered the distance between us.

I cast the 'propel' spell, took careful aim, then launched the axe. It struck the creature between its eyes, stopping it dead in its tracks. The wizards and the headmistress got to it before I did. One of the wizards reached down, and pulled open its pouch. I held my breath, and hardly dared to look.

A small boy's head appeared.

"Tommy!" the headmistress shouted. "Are you all right?"

"I think so, Miss. It smells really bad in here."

The two wizards helped him out. The poor boy was coated in a gooey, smelly substance, but other than that, he appeared to be unharmed.

"Take Tommy inside and get him cleaned up," the headmistress said. "And get this wall repaired before anything else can get through."

The two wizards carried the boy towards the building.

"How did you know about that chute?" the headmistress asked. "I've never seen it before, and I thought I knew most of the secret passageways in CASS."

"I honestly don't know."

"We need to get you back to the airship."

"Can't I stay here and help?"

"There's nothing to be done now except for repairing the wall. The emergency is over, but we'll leave the pupils and staff in their rooms until that's done. I'm afraid we'll have to reschedule your talk. I doubt anyone will be in the mood for it today."

"Don't give it a second thought. I'll be happy to come back again any time."

"Walk with me, Jill. I'll take you back to the playing fields. And thanks again for what you did for Tommy."

Chapter 24

"Planet Earth to Jill!" Jack's voice snapped me out of my daydream.

"Sorry?"

"What's wrong with you this morning?"

"Nothing, I'm not really awake yet."

"I can see that. Look, I should get going. See you tonight." He gave me a peck on the cheek, and was then out of the door.

I could hardly tell him that I'd been thinking about CASS. I still couldn't get my head around everything that had happened. The airship journeys, there and back, hadn't been the ordeal I'd expected, and I hadn't been able to give my talk. But I had rescued a young boy from the clutches of a creature, the likes of which I'd never seen before. I could still see the look on Tommy's face when he'd been pulled out of the pouch. But the thing that was still playing on my mind was the secret passageway—the chute which had allowed me to intercept the pouchfeeder. I'd known exactly where to go, and that pressing the shield would open the wall.

How?

I'd been over and over it in my mind, but it still made no sense. I hadn't even heard of CASS until recently, and I certainly had never been there before. So how had I known the secret passageway was there?

I couldn't afford to dwell on it any longer because today was the day of the NOCA conference. I'd been worried I might find it difficult to hire a clown's costume at such short notice, but it proved not to be a problem.

Presumably, most of the attendees of the conference had their own costumes, and didn't need to hire one.

I changed into it in the outer office before Jules arrived for work.

"Why on earth are you wearing that, Jill?" she said when she walked in.

"I'm going to a clown conference."

"Clowns freak me out." She shuddered.

"Me too. Do you think you could help me with the make-up?"

"I'll try, but I've never really done anything like that before."

Considering it was Jules' first attempt at applying clown make-up, she made a very good job of it. I could barely bring myself to look at my reflection in the mirror because every time I did, it scared me to death.

When I walked through to my office, Winky came out from under the sofa. As soon as he saw me, his fur stood on end, and his tail bushed up. He hissed at me, and then disappeared back under the sofa.

"It's only me, Winky."

He didn't budge.

"You don't have to be scared. It's me."

Nothing I said or did, could persuade him to come back out. I could hardly blame him; I felt the same way about clowns. He was still under there when I went back through to the outer office.

"I'd better get going, Jules."

"Why didn't you get changed there, Jill?"

"I can't run the risk of being recognised."

"Right. Well, good luck."

***

I'd never seen so many clowns in one place as there were at the Washbridge Conference Centre, where the NOCA conference was being held. It was my idea of hell, but I had to go through with it. I'd added my name to the list of attendees when I'd been on Andrew Clowne's computer, so gaining access wasn't a problem.

There were clowns of all shapes and sizes. Fortunately for me, both Don Keigh and Ray Carter were in their everyday clothes. If they'd been dressed as clowns, I'm not sure I would ever have found them.

"It's me—Jill," I said to Don.

"Jill? I had no idea that you'd be here today. I thought the threat was over?"

"There's something that I need you two to hear."

"What are you talking about?" Ray asked.

Without going into details, I convinced them both to hide behind the curtain at the back of the stage. Then, I waited.

About ten minutes later, Andrew Clowne, who was also wearing his everyday clothes, walked onto the stage, and took his seat at the table set out for the three committee members. He was blissfully unaware that his two colleagues were behind the curtain at the back of the stage. That was my cue to act.

I climbed up the steps onto the stage, and walked over to him. I knew that he wouldn't recognise me, but I had to make sure that he didn't recognise my voice either, so I conjured up yet another voice.

"I hope you don't mind me coming up here," I said. "I just wanted to say what an excellent job I think you've done as chairman of NOCA."

"Thank you very much." He beamed. "What's your name?"

"Miss Potty."

"That's a great name."

"Thank you. Why don't you continue in the position of chairman?"

"Unfortunately, the NOCA constitution doesn't allow me to serve another term."

"Is that why you decided to fake the extortion demand?"

He looked stunned. It was time to revert to my normal voice. "You've been siphoning money out of the contingency fund ever since you took over as chairman, haven't you, Andrew?"

"Jill? Is that you?"

"You knew that once the new chairman took over, the game would be up. You had to come up with a plan to account for the missing money."

"That's just rubbish."

"I don't think so. Why else would you send me to pay off the extortionist with a bag full of plain paper?"

"You had no business looking inside the bag."

"But I did, and that's when I realised that there never was an extortionist. You created the letters demanding the money, didn't you? And, you knew that if I left the bag on the bridge, someone would take it sooner or later."

"This is all just speculation. You don't know anything about our accounts."

"That's where you're wrong. While you were at the TV station yesterday, I got to have a good look through all your paperwork, and on your computer." I changed my voice to that of Patricia Delmore, of Clown TV fame. "How did the TV show go, by the way?"

"That was you?"

"It was. While you were away on a wild goose chase, I found all the information I needed to confirm my suspicions. When you first came to see me, you pretended to be dead set against the idea of paying the extortion demand, but secretly you hoped that the two so-called murders would convince your fellow committee members to approve the payment. What could look better than for you to be the only one voting against? But when they didn't approve the payment, you panicked. You had to do something to change their minds, so you used one of the props, which had been confiscated by the Test Lab, to kill poor Mr Bobo."

"This is all very interesting, Jill, but you still don't have a shred of evidence."

"Wrong again. The police have managed to lift a set of fingerprints from the wrapping paper that was on the present you sent to Mr Bobo." I lied.

"It's your fault that Bobo is dead." There was hatred in his eyes. "I never wanted to hurt anyone. If you hadn't persuaded the others to ignore the extortion demand, Bobo would still be alive."

At that moment, Don Keigh and Ray Carter stepped from behind the curtain.

"No, Andrew," Ray Carter said. "It's *your* fault that Bobo is dead. You killed him."

Don Keigh already had his phone in his hand; he was calling the police.

***

I was the last to arrive at Aunt Lucy's house for Grandma's birthday party. Or at least, I was almost the last. There was no sign of the birthday girl herself. Everyone else was seated around the dining room table. Although the room was decorated with balloons, and there were party poppers on the table, there was no party atmosphere. Instead, everyone looked as though they were waiting to be hanged.

"Where's Grandma?" I said, in a hushed voice.

The twins shrugged. Aunt Lucy shook her head. "You tell us."

There was a pile of presents, all a similar shape and size, on the sideboard. I placed mine on top of them.

"Hi, guys," I said to Lester, William and Alan.

They managed a collective grunt in reply. It was obvious that none of them wanted to be there.

"What time is the party meant to start?" I asked.

"Ten minutes before you got here," Pearl said.

My phone vibrated; I had a text message.

"It's from Grandma." I read it aloud, "I have decided to go to bingo instead."

We all looked at one another in disbelief. Even by Grandma's standards, this was outrageous.

"I don't believe it." Aunt Lucy was red in the face. "After all the time I've spent preparing the food, and she decides to go to bingo instead?"

"We spent a fortune on balloons and party poppers," Amber complained.

"And on her present." Pearl sighed.

I was lost for words. Every time I thought Grandma couldn't surprise me again, she managed to do it.

"You lot are so easy to wind up." Grandma cackled, as she walked into the room. "Did you really think I'd miss this happy, family gathering? Where's the drink?"

"I thought we'd eat first." Aunt Lucy got to her feet.

"You thought wrong, then." Grandma went through to the lounge, and moments later came back with a glass of whiskey.

After Aunt Lucy had served the food, the twins picked up their party poppers and pulled the cords. Nothing happened. Alan and William tried theirs with the same result.

"Where did you buy *these* from?" Grandma glared at the twins, after her party popper failed too.

"They were on special offer at Party Express." Pearl was avoiding eye contact with Grandma.

"No wonder."

The meal was superb. Aunt Lucy had made Grandma's favourite: toad in the hole. Not even Grandma could find anything to complain about.

"How's the new job going, Fester?" Grandma asked.

Aunt Lucy looked daggers at Grandma, but said nothing.

"So far, so good," Lester replied.

"Sounds like a bit of a dead-end job to me." Grandma laughed. "Get it? Dead-end job? What's wrong with you lot?"

"Would anyone like dessert?" Aunt Lucy asked.

"Are we going to have some of the twins' invisible cakes?" Grandma cackled again.

The twins exchanged glances, and I saw Amber mouth the words 'how did she know?'

Aunt Lucy's apple pie and custard was delicious. I was

hoping someone else might ask for seconds so I could too, but no one did.

"It's time for the presents, I think," Aunt Lucy said.

"I want to give Grandma my present first," Pearl said.

"No! I want to give her mine first," Amber objected.

The two of them rushed to collect their presents, and then both tried to pass them to Grandma.

"Why don't you open them together for me?" she said.

The twins didn't need telling twice. They both started to tear off the wrapping paper.

Grandma's expression was a picture when she saw what was inside.

"Bunions Away?" Grandma looked from one box to the other identical box.

"It's a revolutionary new treatment," Pearl said.

"I bought mine first!" Amber got in quickly.

"No, you didn't. I did."

"Enough!" Grandma interrupted. "Let's see what Lucy and Jill have bought me."

"You can go first, Jill," Aunt Lucy said.

"No, it's okay. After you."

"Never mind." Grandma stood up. "I'll do it myself." She began to tear the wrapping paper off the two remaining presents.

She now had four bottles of Bunions Away.

"Look at it this way," I said. "You're never likely to run out."

Grandma glared at me. "Now I remember why I don't bother with birthdays." She grabbed her coat. "I really am off to bingo now."

"You forgot your presents!" I called after her.

***

I was totally exhausted by the exploits of the day. If I'd gone straight home, I would probably have fallen asleep, and that would have been it for the evening. So instead, I decided to call in at the office to see if I-Sweat was still open. I figured that a quick workout would wake me up.

As I climbed the stairs, I could see the lights were still on in I-Sweat, so I dropped my bag off in my office, and grabbed my sports gear.

The doors to I-Sweat were open, but there was no one on reception.

"Jill! Hi." It was Gavin. He appeared to be the only person in the gym.

"Hi, Gavin. Sorry, I didn't realise you were closed."

"Officially, we closed ten minutes ago, but I'm just about to do my own workout, so you can stay until I've finished if you like? I'll be here for about thirty minutes."

"Great. That'll be more than enough time. I'll get changed."

I started on one of the rowing machines. Gavin was at the opposite end of the room, lifting weights; he had fastened his long hair up on top of his head. After a few minutes, I swapped to one of the treadmills.

Gavin made me jump when he appeared at my side. The noise from the treadmill had muffled his footsteps.

"Sorry, Jill, I didn't mean to scare you."

"It's okay. Are you ready to go home?"

"Not just yet. I'm okay for another fifteen minutes or so."

As he walked away, I caught his reflection in the mirror on the wall. That's when I saw it. A small tattoo, on the nape of his neck, in the shape of a goblet.

I almost fell off the treadmill. My heart was racing but not because of the running—I was terrified. All this time I'd assumed the witchfinder was weird Mr Kilbride, when in fact it was Gavin.

I started to make my way slowly towards the exit, but Gavin must have sensed my movement because he turned around. He glanced at the mirror, and realised that the game was up. His ever-permanent smile disappeared.

"There's no point in trying to get away, Jill. It's over."

"I don't think so!"

I rushed out of the door, and slammed it shut, but seconds later, I heard it open again. He was only a few feet behind me as I rushed along the corridor and into my office. I had to get to my bag, which contained the syringes of Brewflower. I managed to grab it off my desk, and pull out the white box, but before I could take one out, Gavin had rugby tackled me to the ground. The box slid across the floor and out of reach. I cast the 'power' spell and tried to push him off me, but he just laughed.

"Your magic doesn't work on me, witch! And soon you won't be around for it to work on anyone else."

This was it. There was nothing I could do. I was a goner.

"Jill! Catch!" Winky threw one of the syringes to me.

I caught it, and stuck it into Gavin's thigh.

He stared at the syringe in disbelief, but then fell off me. I managed to pull myself up into a sitting position. For the next few minutes, nothing happened, but then Gavin, or whatever his name really was, stood up, and walked out of the room.

I was alive! I was still alive!

"Boy, do you owe me big time." Winky grinned.

ALSO BY ADELE ABBOTT

The Witch P.I. Mysteries:

Witch Is When... (Books #1 to #12)
Witch Is When It All Began
Witch Is When Life Got Complicated
Witch Is When Everything Went Crazy
Witch Is When Things Fell Apart
Witch Is When The Bubble Burst
Witch Is When The Penny Dropped
Witch Is When The Floodgates Opened
Witch Is When The Hammer Fell
Witch Is When My Heart Broke
Witch Is When I Said Goodbye
Witch Is When Stuff Got Serious
Witch Is When All Was Revealed

Witch Is Why... (Books #13 to #24)
Witch Is Why Time Stood Still
Witch is Why The Laughter Stopped
Witch is Why Another Door Opened
Witch is Why Two Became One
Witch is Why The Moon Disappeared
Witch is Why The Wolf Howled
Witch is Why The Music Stopped
Witch is Why A Pin Dropped
Witch is Why The Owl Returned
Witch is Why The Search Began
Witch is Why Promises Were Broken
Witch is Why It Was Over

The Susan Hall Mysteries:
Whoops! Our New Flatmate Is A Human.
Whoops! All The Money Went Missing.
Whoops! There's A Canary In My Coffee
See web site for availability.

AUTHOR'S WEB SITE
http:www.AdeleAbbott.com

FACEBOOK
http://www.facebook.com/AdeleAbbottAuthor

MAILING LIST
(new release notifications only)
http:/AdeleAbbott.com/adele/new-releases/

Printed in Great Britain
by Amazon